GUNS

OF THE WASTE LAND:

DEPARTURE

Leverett Butts

Hold Fast Press
Long Beach, CA

DEDICATION

For Laura:

This may be the closest to a fantasy I write.
I wish you could read it. I think you'd like it.

Prologue

What the Women Saw

I.

Twenty years ago…

The settlement was small, consisting only of a small adobe hut and a stone well, both beneath the spreading branches of a giant Yucca tree. As the sun rose over the structure, three women emerged. All three had dusky skin and wore leather dresses topped with vests of colorful beaded fabric. The first woman was young, in her late twenties or early thirties, perhaps, with raven-dark hair, and carried a small wooden spinning wheel. The second was perhaps twenty years older with hair a charcoal gray. She carried a basket of wool and cotton, and the third, the oldest had snowy-white hair and could have been anywhere between seventy and a hundred and three. She carried what appeared to be a long, folded, multi-colored shawl.

They set their baskets and the wheel down at the base of the tree, and while the two older women began sorting the material into separate piles, the youngest, Ałk'idáá, went to the well and turned the crank lowering a bucket to draw water. When she had

1

raised it again, the middle-aged woman, Kut, brought one of the empty baskets over, and her younger companion filled it with water from the bucket. The older woman, Náásgóó, then began a low keening chant as Kut circled the trunk of the tree, slowly pouring water on its roots. When this was done, all three women bowed to the tree and turned to the piles of wool and cotton.

Ałk'idáá turned the basket over and sat upon it beside the wheel and began feeding strands of both materials into the wheel as she worked the pedal steadily with her feet. As she spun, Kut began pulling the yarn directly from the bobbin and with a dizzying dexterity began knitting it into cloth sheets that Ałk'idáá, with the same dexterous skill, would sew onto the shawl.

"Tell me," Kut said as she knit her fabric, "What do you see?"

II.

Gettysburg, Pennsylvania
July, 1863

Ida Alkaev, the young Russian seamstress clad in a brown dress
and beaded vest, sat outside the commander's tent mending his
jacket as well as she could. It was slow work. The scarcity of
good thread through the Confederate forces forced her to make
do with the thinnest hemp twine she could beg from the
quartermaster. Invoking General Drake's name helped, but only
insofar as what little Jenkins had in his stores was made available
for her, and there was little enough left after the rest of the
brigade had done their own meager repairs to their saddles, tents,
and bedding.

   As she worked a large needle through the left shoulder of the
Drake's jacket, she heard the slow, steady footsteps of the camp
minister approach. She looked up, twine clenched between her
teeth and smiled.

   "Good evening, Miss Ida," the preacher said quietly, nodding.
"How are you this evening?"

   "*Privyet*, Merle," she replied around the twine. "My hands were
very … sore tonight and my fingers were acting older than me."

   "Have you been to Doc Todd's tent? He may have a salve."

   "Bah!" Ida spat the twine out of her mouth and glared at
Merle. "Doktor Tott did not know, how do you say, his bottom
from a bung hole. I left a tea poultice waiting for me in my tent."

   "I will pray for you," Merle said, and Ida chuckled. "Is he in?"

   Ida pushed the needle through the shoulder and the twine
came through without ripping the fabric any more. She nodded
absently, then gasped harshly. Her shoulders went rigid and her
head snapped up as if someone had jerked her by her black
bangs.

   "Ida?" Merle fell to one knee and placed both hands on either
side of her face. Her eyes stared beyond him, but he could at

3

least feel her even breaths on his face and knew she had not died. "Ida?" He repeated. "Can you hear me?"

"Coyote always took many guises," she said, still staring beyond Merle toward the horizon and the lowering sun. "Since the beginning of time, he had no love for us, and lapped up our suffering like river water."

[She speaks the truth in her fashion; listen to her] It was a voice Merle had heard his entire life, but it never ceased to startle him. He shuddered and looked over his shoulder despite the fact that he knew where the voice came from. It sounded like his voice, but he knew it wasn't.

Ida was still staring blankly in the darkness. Merle waved his fingers in front of her face, but her eyes remained fixed. He grabbed her shoulders and shook her gently. "Miss Ida, come back to me." When this got no response he snapped his fingers rapidly inches from her eyes.

At this, Ida blinked, shook her head, and met Merle's eyes. "You should not have allowed this," She said. Then she rose, folded the jacket under her arm, rolled the twine and needle into her apron pocket, and walked away. Merle noticed a beaded design on the back of her vest: a young crow pulling itself from a fractured egg. "I have finished for the night. It all began here, and you should have stopped him."

[Better do what she says, boy. Stop him.]

"We are to march with Pickett tomorrow." Luther said over his shoulder. Merle sat at Luther's desk flipping cards idly and setting them criss-cross in piles of three in front of him. At first it was all he could do; Luther did little but stare into the flame of the lantern sitting upon the small table by his cot and sip from an earthenware jug he held loosely at his side. Merle had already made five piles, before Luther even spoke. "The ridge is well defended, but Lee believes we can take it." At this Luther turned to face Merle. "I am going to die tomorrow," he said. "I can feel it in the pit of my belly."

Merle flipped a card and began a sixth pile. The seven of clubs.
[He'll survive, but he will not be the same. Tell him no.]

4

"You won't die," he said patiently. "I'm sure Lee has the whole maneuver planned to last footstep. You'll be fine."

"God tell you that, Merle?" Luther gave a humorless chuckle. "Because otherwise you are as full of shit as an oat-stuffed mule."

"Maybe," Merle said absently spinning the card with his finger. "I feel it in my gut, too. And my gut," at this Merle smiled with a look to Luther's jug, "is a damned sight more pristine than yours."

"Well, you cannot deny that I may die."

Merle said nothing, he simply flipped another card to lay across the previous.

Luther took another swig, belched, and swayed a little. His voice, however, lost none of its vigor. "I must see Ingrid," he said. "Tonight."

Two of spades.

[This is not a good idea, Merle.]

Merle stared directly at Luther. "We have talked about this. It is not a good idea. She is married."

Luther turned from his friend walked to the tent-flap, looking out. "She wasn't always."

"That does not even make sense, Luther."

Luther appeared not to have heard. "If Cornwallis cared a thing for her, she would not be anywhere near this godforsaken battlefield."

"None of this matters," Merle began nervously shuffling the remaining cards in his hands. "What matters is that you cannot do this thing. She is another man's wife regardless of what you think of that man's safeguarding abilities."

"I am doing it, Merle."

"He is a Yankee Colonel, Luther. How on God's green earth do you intend to get past our pickets, much less theirs."

"Corporal Alson is scouting a way for me."

[Coyote laps up our suffering like water.]

Merle sighed. "Well, if you have this all planned out, why did you call for me?"

"I wanted to confess to you."

5

"Luther..." Merle was momentarily dumbstruck. He took a breath and began again. "Luther, you cannot ask forgiveness for a sin you intend to commit."

"Then come with me, and I will ask forgiveness when the sin has been committed."

"I cannot go with you as a spiritual advisor with sure knowledge of your intent to commit adultery, Luther." Merle's voice came as an exasperated sigh as he all but slammed a nine of hearts on the latest pile, [*Wishes fulfilled often have dreadful consequences*] and then swept the entire tableau onto the floor. "It does not work that way."

Luther looked out of his tent then stepped back holding the flap open, allowing a corporal to enter. He carried three dark oiled-canvas ponchos. Luther looked again at his friend. "Then come with me as a friend."

Luther looked to the newcomer. "Come in Corporal Alson; just put those over there." He motioned to his cot in the corner.

The corporal looked rangy and unkempt, like a dog left out long enough to go feral. He had stringy charcoal hair that hung in his face and at least a three days' growth of stubble. He had clearly seen his share of battle, though: a scar on his right cheek, where a bullet had apparently grazed him in some previous skirmish, pulled his mouth open, giving him a permanent sneer. He moved to the cot and dropped the ponchos there. Underneath the ponchos, he carried three firearms: two revolvers and Spencer repeater.

"Got us some Yankee guns," he said as he piled the revolvers on the ponchos and leaned the rifle against the cot. "The two what had'em won't be needin'em no more."

"Thank you, Jack," Luther said. "I believe my Colts will suffice, though I do not believe we will need them. Still, best to be safe." He turned then to Merle. "Well, then Reverend," he gave Merle a grave look. "Will you join us? At least to keep me out of trouble?"

The voice spoke in his head again. [*Do not let that man do this thing.*]

Perhaps, Merle thought, *I can dissuade him en route.*

6

[Sure.]

Merle glared at his friend, then sighed heavily, walked to the cot, and grabbed a poncho and the rifle. "Damn you, Luther," he swore. "For the love of God and all that's holy, do not make me regret this more than I already do."

Luther only grinned and slapped Merle's back. "Come along, Jack," he called over his shoulder to the corporal as he led Merle out of his tent. "Time tarries for none of us, and we have a big day tomorrow."

The three men moved as cautiously as they could through the camp. A mist had risen earlier in the evening, helping to hide them as they moved into the enemy camp, but lacking rain, the ponchos seemed more of a hindrance. Yes, the dark color helped them blend into the night, but the warm air of midsummer turned positively smothering inside the heavily rubberized garments. Merle half hoped he would collapse in exhaustion, and bring the entire venture to a premature close, but he did not.

"Luther," Merle whispered after they moved past the Confederate sentries, "please consider this. You are putting your men in peril if we are caught, and for what? A fleeting tumble in a married woman's petticoats?"

Jack Alson, who had slunk ahead and was scouting their way, looked back and hissed for them to be silent.

Luther ignored him. "Have you ever been in love, Merle?" He stopped to look his friend square in the face. "I mean truly and wholly in love, and with a woman you could never have?"

Merle wanted to say he had, but he knew, too, that Luther, who had known him for the better part of both their lives, would see the lie and knew the answer anyway.

"No, Luther, I have not ever been in love."

Luther chuckled grimly then patted his friends shoulder companionably. "Then regardless of your skill in all things spiritual, you have nothing more to say on this matter," he whispered, moving forward to join his corporal, "You cannot possibly understand my pain, Merle."

They moved along the outskirts of the Yankee encampment past Leister's Farm and General Meade's headquarters, keeping just inside the tree line, until they came near Cemetery Ridge and Col. Cornwallis' encampment. The camp seemed strangely empty. There had been fighting all day, and both sides had supposedly retired leaving only sentries to prevent an ambush, but Cornwallis and his men seemed to be nowhere in sight.

"Are you sure he is away, Jack?" Luther asked his corporal.

The younger man sniffed the air tentatively, then turned to his commander. "Yes," he growled lowly, "I sent some of the pack away east to harry the sentries. He should be gone for another," at this Corporal Alson glanced at the moon, "hour at least."

"Very well," Luther nodded, and glanced through the tent flaps. "You two stand guard. And Merle?"

Merle glanced at him, but said nothing.

"God will have mercy on me. You have never known what it is to love a woman. Given his unorthodox relationship with Mary, surely he understands a man's heart more than you do."

[Yes, and that is indeed the problem.]

Merle sighed and turned back to scan the tree line. He would occasionally glance toward the tent flap when the murmur of Luther's conversation broke his attention. Once he thought he saw a crib with a small child grasping the bars when the southerly breeze whipped the flap a bit. After a few minutes, however, when the murmurs of conversation grew to sighs and moans and finally snores, Merle understood that for better or worse, the die had been cast.

He looked about for Corporal Alson, but could see no trace of him.

Where'd that son of a bitch go? Merle asked himself. *I never saw him leave.*

[You're more perceptive than you know, Merle.] The strange voice seemingly arose from the rising mist. *[You should listen to yourself more often.]*

Off in the distance near the tree line and the Yankee sentries, he heard some yelling, what sounded like a pack of dogs barking, then a few isolated shots. To his left just in shadow he spied what looked like a small wolf slinking around the perimeter, but when he looked again, it was gone.

Later he heard snuffling from behind the tent. When he crept around to check, he caught sight of the snuffling canine figure again sniffing underneath the fringe of the canvas tent, but the slim stream of lantern light leaking from the seams showed that the animal had no fur. Indeed, it seemed almost to have scales, like a snake or a lizard. Merle could never be sure of what he saw because the creature did not remain long to be admired, but took off quick as lightning when Merle turned the corner.

"What are you staring at?" The voice came from just out of Merle's field of vision. It was the low growling voice of Jack Alson.

"There was a strange beast here snuffling under the tent," Merle whispered. "It ran off when I approached. It must have gone right past you not twenty seconds ago."

Alson stepped into the dim light, adjusting his poncho and shrugging. "I saw nothing," he replied, "but we best be waking the Colonel." He nodded in the direction of the sentry line beyond Merle. "Cornwallis is coming back. He seems to have discovered our ruse, and is none too happy."

Merle felt his stomach fall, and gripped his rifle tightly. "What do you mean 'discovered our ruse'?"

"His men caught one of my pack." Alson spoke with the same nonchalance as if he had mentioned stepping in dung as he crossed a cow field. "Shot him dead, but Cornwallis is no fool. He will know this was a distraction."

As if on cue, Merle heard voices in the distance behind him, excited, and coming closer. Alson waved his hand inside the tent. "Colonel," He said more loudly, "it is time to leave."

Merle could hear the sound of Luther rousing himself quickly and pulling his clothes back on. In a matter of mere moments, Luther was leaving the tent as a young woman with red hair unpinned and grasping a shawl around otherwise bare shoulders followed.

"Will I see you again?" her voice had something of lilt to it.

"If God grants me safe passage tomorrow," Luther said. "I swear, Ingrid, I will come for you and Mordecai. Your husband be damned." Then he kissed her on the forehead and gently pushed back within the tent.

By now the voices were nearer. Merle could make out actual phrases.

"...diversion," one voice explained.

"...drive us away from camp," another added.

Merle turned to his friend. "Luther," he said, failing to keep his voice steady as his anxiety rose, "we need to leave now."

Luther nodded and drew his revolvers. "Where is Corporal Alson?"

[That's a good question, Merle. Do you have an answer for him?]

Merle looked around, sure enough, the corporal had slunk away into the shadows again. "I don't know, but we cannot worry about it now." Merle's voice rose in pitch. "Cornwallis and his men are coming."

"Is that them?" inquired a third voice seemingly immediately behind Merle. He jerked around to find himself confronted by two men in uniforms so dark they faded into the night. One was no more than fourteen or fifteen while the other, an officer, was significantly older.

Without thinking, Merle fired his rifle blindly as he heard Luther fire his revolvers from behind. Both men fell without so much as a whimper. From inside the tent the woman screamed and a baby began wailing into the night, though the sound was considerably muffled by the ringing in Merle's ears.

He stood dumbfounded as Luther stepped past him and levelled one colt to the officer's temple and pulled the trigger then did the same to the younger man lying to the officer's side. Neither gun made a sound that Merle could hear despite the fire leaping from the muzzles and the heads shattered in the blast.

Merle had the sensation of teeth pulling his sleeve, and when he turned around he found Alson returned and pulling his arm in the direction of the tree line. Luther was already running ahead.

"Run, you damned fool," Alson growled, and Merle heard these words perfectly clearly despite his deafness. "It's too late

10

for salvation, Padre. You're in it, and if you do not run, you will hang."

Merle ran.

It seemed as if the shadows of the tree line melded with the mist that had been gathering all evening and enveloped the three men as they ran. As his ears quit ringing, Merle heard the sounds of pursuit. He even heard the cracks of rifles firing into the woods, but none ever came close to him. He was swallowed by a darkness that hid him and his companions from view as they made their way back over the sentry lines and into their own camp.

By the time they reached Luther's camp, Jack Alson had once again disappeared somewhere along the way. Merle sank to the ground outside Luther's tent, in the spot where Miss Ida had mended Luther's jacket. That seemed to have been weeks ago.

"I killed a boy," Merle gasped. "Luther, I have committed murder."

"And I have slain my rival, Merle." Luther bent down to pat his friend's shoulder. "There's nothing can change that now. Comfort yourself in the knowledge that they both would have killed you were you the slower on the trigger."

"We shouldn't have been there!" Merle screamed and felt his voice breaking. "It was a fool's errand to go, and I told you as much. Had you listened, that boy would still be living."

Luther rose from his friend and made to enter his tent. "Perhaps he would have died tomorrow." Luther said moving the flap aside. "However, Cornwallis would also be alive, and my way to Ingrid obstructed."

Merle stared dumbfounded at his friend as he stepped inside the tent and let the flap fall close. "All-in-all a fair trade," Luther said from within the tent. "Now go get some sleep, Merle. We take Cemetery Ridge tomorrow."

Merle slowly rose and moved to his own quarters a few tents down from Luther. When he entered, he fell immediately to his knees, and propped himself by his cot.

"Almighty God," he prayed aloud, "who does freely pardon all who repent and turn to Him, now fulfill in my own contrite heart the promise of redeeming grace; forgiving my sin, and cleansing me from an evil conscience; through the perfect sacrifice of Christ Jesus our Lord. Amen."

He remained there in supplication, but received no comfort. Presently he tried again.

"Gracious God," he began again, "my sin is too heavy to carry, too real to hide, and too deep to undo. Forgive what my lips tremble to name, what my hearts can no longer bear. Set me free from a past I cannot change; open to me a future in which I can be changed; and grant me grace to grow more and more in your likeness and image, through Jesus Christ, the light of the world. Amen."

Still he felt no relief.

"Are you there, God?"

There was no answer, nor would there ever be again.

III.

"Tell me," Kut said as she knit her fabric, "What do you see?"

Alk'idáá narrowed her eyes on the thread as it made its way around the wheel and onto the bobbin. "I saw changes, Mother," she said. "The world shook and Yucca wept. Coyote tricked the Human Beings into turning upon each other."

Kut nodded and stared at the fabric she wove. "I, too, see this," she said. "It happens now, just as before. Coyote is not to be trusted, but Human Beings are prideful. They think that they cannot be fooled by lesser animals or nature."

IV.

Fighting Bear had been gone one moon before Hachi-Mahal, Stream Woman, discovered her courses no longer ran. She told herself at first that it was of no concern. They had forgotten a course once or twice since she had become a woman; this was not necessarily a sign of anything of note. When the next moon waxed and waned and there were still no more courses, she knew that a change was on the wind.

She knew of an herb-woman who lived a day's walk from the hogan in which she lived with her father, Michaa Odjig, and the next morning, packing only enough provisions to last her the day into a deerskin bag she wore at her hip and saying nothing to her father, Hachi-Mahal set off into the Waste Lands seeking the herb-woman to ask her advice.

She found the herb-woman after only a few hours on the trail. The woman knelt haunches-on-heels by a small stream collecting water in a pail that never seemed to fill. She would lay the pail on its side in the stream and allow water to flow into it, but when she removed it, the pail would be empty. She tried it again and got the same result. Though her leather dress frequently dipped into stream, it, too, seemed to repel water as did the fringes of her beaded vest. On her third attempt, the woman became aware of Hachi-Mahal approaching, so she set the pail down without looking in it. Hachi-Mahal noticed that this time the pail was full to the brim.

"Greetings, Hachi-Mahal," the woman said rising from her crouch and tucking a loose strand of charcoal hair behind her ear. "It is far too hot a day for a woman in your condition to be traveling."

Hachi-Mahal stared at the woman dumbfounded. "How do you know of me and my condition?"

14

"I know a great many things that are," the woman replied, and she crossed the stream, approaching Hachi-Mahal. "Though by no means all." She placed her hand upon Hachi-Mahal's belly and rubbed a circle clockwise around her navel. "I do not know, for example," she began rubbing counterclockwise, "who has put this in your belly. Someone of great power and fate, that is clear." The woman then held her hand to her face and inhaled. "Fighting Bear?"

"It was the harvest king," Hachi-Mahal replied.

"Ah," the woman chuckled softly, "and the harvest king is who? Fighting Bear?

"I chose the strongest and bravest warrior in our settlement."

"I see you have learned well the art of answering questions, child." The old woman leaned in and sniffed Hachi-Mahal's face. "You are as wily as a fish, a worthy scion of Michaa Odjig. Perhaps one day the child in your belly is to rise as high as his grandfather and lead your people, too."

"So I carry a boy? He will be chief after my father?"

The woman shrugged. "You carry a manchild, beyond that I cannot say. Ask me in twenty years, or find my mother and ask her."

The woman gave Hachi-Mahal's belly a final pat and turned to return to her pail. On the back of the woman's vest, Hachi-Mahal could make out the shape of a black bird flying over a flat landscape. When she got to the middle of the stream, the woman turned around and regarded Hachi-Mahal, who was now absently rubbing her own belly. "In seven more moons, look for me at your hogan. Together we can bring your son into the world and see what can be seen."

When the woman reached her pail, she let out a frustrated sigh and held it up. It was empty. "This is not the correct water." She said. "I must keep looking." Then she turned and began walking toward the horizon. Hachi-Mahal reached into her hip bag and removed a strip of dried venison, and when she looked back up, the woman was nowhere to be seen.

There was not enough light for her to reach the hogan, so when she had covered about half the distance home and the sun was westering, she made camp beneath a large yucca tree. She gathered kindling and firewood from the ground, removed two flint stones from her pouch and set to work sparking a fire.

"It is late in the evening for a young woman to be out alone," the voice came from just outside her field of vision, so she looked up from the kindling to see a coyote sitting on the opposite side of the fire ring. It tilted its head quizzically from the right. "If I may share your fire, I will protect you from predators." The coyote's mouth did not move, but the voice was as clear as her own.

"I have always heard," she said, "that coyotes were the dangerous predators in the desert."

"Coyotes are dangerous, it is true," the voice almost seemed to be coming from the very air around her, "but we are not by any means the only predators. If you share your fire, and perhaps the meat in your pouch with me, I will protect you this night as if you were part of my own pack."

Hachi-Mahal thought about this. Coyotes were treacherous animals, it was true, but better, she thought, to have a coyote in sight than in the shadows. She reached into her pouch and tossed a slice of venison to her companion. He caught it in mid-air with his mouth. "That seems acceptable," she said, "so long as you swear by Great Sky Father that you will not betray me this night and will protect me from all harm, even from yourself."

The coyote bowed his head until his nose touched the dry dust of the ground. "I swear by Great Sky Father and by Father Yucca," the voice said earnestly, "that I will not harm you by thought or action this night."

"And in the morning we will go our separate ways each unhindered by the other?"

"Of course."

"Then you may share my fire."

The two sat by the fire each chewing a piece of venison. The coyote would occasionally sniff the air and look in the direction

16

of Hachi-Mahal, but he would remain silent. After a few minutes of this Hachi-Mahal sighed in irritation.

"What is it?" She asked the beast. "What do you smell."

"You are with child," the beast answered and sniffed again. "A manchild."

"So I have been told," Hachi-Mahal said. "What of it?"

"Will you tell him his father is Fighting Bear, or will you tell him his father is Dog Man?"

"I will tell him," she replied, "that his father is the harvest king."

"That is probably best." The coyote swallowed the last of his venison. "Such a boy does not need to know his true father. Much better to be the son of a god. Is there any more of that meat?"

Hachi-Mahal tossed her last piece of venison and again the coyote caught it in his mouth. "You think I should tell him who his father is?"

"I think," the coyote said after swallowing his meat, "that an ordinary boy needs to know his father. He needs a man to emulate, or else how will he know to walk upright and to speak true? How will he know the proper way to hunt deer and to make war with his enemies? A harvest child, though…" at this the coyote paused to give his next words emphasis. "A harvest child knows that he is half divine and has no need to know his earthly father. He will grow to be a strong leader because he knows his father will not have the same frailties as a mortal man. He will not have the wanderlust of Fighting Bear, nor will he have the resentment of Dog Man. Perhaps he will even be chosen harvest king in his own right."

Hachi-Mahal knew that coyotes often spoke falsely, but this coyote had taken an oath against thoughts and deeds.

But not words, she told herself.

True, but thoughts create words, she retorted, *One cannot speak falsely without thinking falsely. In this, coyote can be trusted.*

Perhaps…

That was seven moons ago. Today, Hachi-Mahal woke and knew it was time. She rose from her pallet, pressing both hands into the small of her back and waddled outside the hogan. Before she was born, her father had raised this hogan next to the stream that ran through the Aticota land, befitting a man who enjoyed fishing as much as Michaa Odjig. He was the only man in the village who could catch fish with his bare hands. Hachi-Mahal always wondered as a girl if this was why he was chosen as chief.

Now, though, she knew better. Michaa Odjig was also one of the wisest men in the tribe and often consulted even by other tribes for his counsel. Many claimed that it was Michaa Odjig alone who had kept the tribes from war for the last few decades.

Hachi-Mahal went to the stream to splash water in her face, but she found her father sitting on the edge of the stream wiggling his toes in the water talking with the herb woman.

"Today is a great day, my daughter," Michaa Odjig said when he saw Hachi-Mahal approach. "Kut, here, has come to bring your son to us."

Hachi-Mahal bowed to the herb woman. "I thank you," she said and as she did so a movement on the other side of the stream caught her eye. A beast on all fours, like a dog, but with dark scaly skin like a lizard ran behind a stand of scrub bush. It happened so quickly, though, Hachi-Mahal was unsure whether she had seen truly or whether it was the dregs of a dream. She shook her head to clear the image from her mind, and knelt down in the stream to splash her face.

As she did so, she felt a pressure inside her release and felt water streaming down her thighs instead of up.

"It appears," the herb woman said, "that I have arrived just in time." She rose and moved to help Hachi-Mahal up as her father rushed to his daughter's other side to assist as well. "Come, girl," she said soothingly, but glancing across the stream at the stand of scrub, "Let us go inside where it is warm and dry. We need to begin."

It had been a difficult delivery, the boy had come backwards, a bad sign according to the herb woman, but had also been cawled, a good sign.

"This boy is a natural born world shaker," the herb woman said, laying him aside on a pile of buffalo robes as soon as she saw he was breathing normally and turning her attention to Hachi-Mahal, whose blood ran freely as a result of the breached birth.

"Will I be well?" Hachi-Mahal gasped, clenching her teeth in pain. "Will I see my son grow to a man?"

"If I stop this bleeding," the medicine woman said from between Hachi-Mahal's thighs, "you may. Beyond that only Great Sky Father and my mother know."

One hour after the birth and twelve hours since her waters flowed, Hachi-Mahal lay back on her pallet, cradling her newborn son in her arms. The herb woman had only just left, having remained long enough to clean the mess.

"You may not move from the pallet for three days," she had explained when Hachi-Mahal made to rise and help, "or the boy will grow stunted and weak."

"Call my father, then."

The woman snorted derisively. "This is no place for a man, girl. Vomit may be easier to clean than blood, but the smell lingers far longer."

Now Hachi-Mahal lay back, feeding the child while she listened to her father reciting a soft chant for health and prosperity. She slowly became aware of a snuffling just on the other side of the wall by which she rested. It sounded like an animal, a dog maybe, but it had to be huge if its breathing could be heard through the thick adobe walls.

"Congratulations on your manchild, Hachi-Mahal." It was the coyote from so many months ago. "I can smell that he will grow into a strong warrior and a great leader of men."

Hachi-Mahal smiled down at her son suckling at her breast. "A natural born world-shaker," she said.

"Indeed," the coyote agreed. "Remember, though, a god's son need not know his earthly father's name. It will only weaken him and cause him doubt. He is the child of gods, the harvest prince. Let him take pride in…"

The coyote's words were cut off as Michaa Odjig entered the hogan and walked to his daughter. As he bent to brush her black hair behind her ears, Hachi-Mahal heard the shuffling of the coyote as he moved away from the hogan. Michaa Odjig seemed unaware of the sound.

"Have you thought of what we shall name the child, my daughter?"

"No, father," Hachi-Mahal replied, removing the babe from her breast and moving a buffalo hide to cover herself. "I was going to ask you."

At this the shuffling diminished in intensity. Hachi looked at the door of the hogan, half afraid the coyote would appear (*Or something worse*, Hachi-Mahal thought, remembering the leathery-skinned beast she had seen earlier). Instead a small, red fox-like animal sniffed tentatively at the door and crept slowly inside.

Hachi-Mahal nudged her father and nodded at the door. When Michaa Odig saw the animal he chuckled to himself.

"A marten," he said with a note of surprise.

At the sound of Michaa Odjig's voice, the marten jerked his head up, jumped and spun his body in midair, and ran from the door. After it was out of sight, Hachi-Mahal heard a deep growl, followed by a tiny, terrified screech. Then nothing.

Again Michaa Odjig seemed not to hear. "You do not see martens this far south," he said. "It is a sign. We shall name the boy Apistanewj."

A sign, yes, Hachi-Mahal thought, thinking of the fate implied by the growl and the screech. *But of what?*

V.

"Coyote is not to be trusted," Kut said as she wove the fabric from the thread that Ałk'idáá spun, "but Human Beings are prideful. They think that they cannot be fooled by lesser animals or nature."

Ałk'idáá chuckled but with little mirth. "Coyote has always been a trickster," she said.

"It will always be as it was and as it is." Náásgóó added.

VI.

The Waste Lands
Between Bretton and the Aticota Territory

Michaa Odjig does not move as he once did. In his youth, he could walk as fast as many braves rode on horseback. Now, however, he moves slowly and only with the help of a stick. He jokes with his daughter, herself entering her evening years, that he often delays turtles that have the misfortune to get behind him. Increasingly he finds it hard to believe that it was only a few years back that he met the young fool at the stream and gave him a lesson in spear-fishing.

If he had asked the question then, he often finds himself thinking, *things may have turned out differently.*

But the fool did not ask any questions and the evening ended, and time marched on in its appointed path. And its appointed path leads him here. To confront his grandson and persuade him to abandon his own foolish path.

He had been awakened this morning by a strange wisened hand shaking him vigorously.

"Will you not waken, Michaa ODjig?" The voice was that of an old woman, and Michaa Odjig knew who it was immediately.

He rolled over to see a woman with snow white hair turn her back to him and reach for his walking stick. She wore a tanned leather dress over which a beaded vest worked in blue, white, and black beads, depicting an old raven falling to the ground. "What do you want, Náásgóó?" He said, blinking and rubbing his eyes. "And speak plainly. In the seventy summers I have known you, you have ever spoken in riddles."

"You will need to speak to your grandson," she implored, handing him his stick.

Another voice spoke from outside the hogan, this time the voice of a much younger woman "He listened too long to Coyote."

22

A third voice, older than the second but less mature than the first chimed in from the opposite end of the hogan. "Now he plans something terrible."

Michaa Odjig took the proffered stick from Náásgóó and rose slowly to his feet, spine cracking loudly as he did so. He looked at the middle-aged woman in the hogan "Where is his mother, Kut?"

"Not here," Kut replied, "and she is of little use to us in any regard where Apistanewj is concerned."

The younger woman in the doorway sniffed derisively. "She was never any good at keeping him in line. She should have told her son about his heritage, but she listened to Coyote, too."

Kut went to the larder and removed some dried strips of meat, bringing them over to the old man. "He only listens to you, Michaa Odjig. Eat this and be on your way. Follow the sun to find him."

"He may not listen to even you though," Náásgóó added as Michaa Odjig waved the jerky away. "He will always be unreasonable where Fighting Bear and the future of The People are concerned."

"And this concerns them both." Kut again thrust the meat at the old man and this time he took it irritably. "Speak plainly, women!" He grumbled. "What is it he has in mind? What has Coyote convinced him to do?"

"Ghost Dance," all three said together.

Michaa Odjig hears them long before he sees them. A singing chant accentuated by a regular dull beat comes on the dry breeze just as the sun begins to set.

> *He'e'yo'!*
> *Heyo'hänä' Häe'yo!*
> *The sun's beams are running out—He'e'yo'!*
> *The sun's rays are running out—Ahi'ni'yo'!*
> *Yani'tsini'hawa'na!*
> *We shall live again.*

23

Michaa Odjig sighs, takes a pull from his water bladder, and moves in the direction of the voices, just over a rise at least an hour's walk ahead of him.

As he crests the rise an hour later, he sees a ring of men, women, and even small children dancing around a single figure. Not just Aticota dancers either, he sees Commanche and Apache. There are even Cree and Chippewa from the far north; he also sees Lakota and Cherokee.

The dancers move around the central figure first one direction then the other. Though the sun has not completely set, fires have been lit at the four compass points, causing the dancers to cast elongated shadows and to make the individual faces hard, though not impossible, to discern. At first, Michaa Odjig assumes the figure in the center of the circle is Apistanewj, but then he sees his grandson dancing in the ring beside Falling Bird. He is wearing traditional buckskin leggings and moccasins but no shirt. Instead a beaded breastplate with two columns of horizontal pipe beads hangs from his neck to his just above his waist. There is a pattern of some sort running vertically between the two beaded panels, but it is too far away for Michaa Odjig to see clearly. Despite Apistanewj's traditional dress, he still wears his black hair short, in the white man's manner.

The dancing shadows make the man in the middle of the dancing ring hard to pin down. At first he seems to be an older Lakota man with graying hair hanging loose beneath a charcoal colored felt hat and wearing dungarees and a cotton shirt and barefoot. At one point, Michaa Odjig would swear that the figure in the center resembles nothing so much as a shaven canine on its hind legs, but only for an instant. When Michaa Odjig looks again, though, the dancing shadows make the man appear much younger with thick black hair in two braids hanging down each shoulder. He hears leather leggings, tunic, and moccasins all worked in red, orange, and white embroidery. Orange war paint circles both his eyes. Sometimes he seems like a giant tand and orange spider, waving its many arms in time with the chant.

"Greetings Michaa Odjig," Falling Bird cries when he spies the old man. "Come! Dance with us! We are bringing the Spirit World."

"I am much too old to dance, Falling Bird," Michaa Odjig makes a show of dragging his left foot more than usual. "I came to see my grandson."

Falling Bird laughs and slaps Apistanewj, nodding in Michaa Odjig's direction. "Look, boy. See who has come to dance with us."

At this the old man smiles and shakes his head while waving his hands dismissively. "I am too old now. I will see the Spirit World on my own soon enough. I have no wish to see it sooner. I only wish to speak to Apistanewj. We will not be long."

By now, though, Falling Bird has danced out of earshot and Apistanewj has left the ring.

"Take my arm, Grandfather," he says as he moves to Michaa Odjig's left and offers his right elbow. The pattern on his breastplate is clear now: a red skeleton dancing with a black warrior on a field of green. The old man switches his walking stick to his other hand and takes the proffered arm; then the two men move to the edge of the firelight away from the commotion of the dancing and chanting.

"Tell me, Grandfather," Apistanewj asks when they have moved far enough from the ring to speak without yelling and are sitting upon the ground. "Why have you come if not to dance the Ghost Dance with us?"

Michaa Odjig's voice turns to stone. "I have come to stop my imprudent grandson from bringing disaster on us all. You must stop this foolishness." At this, he boxes his grandson's ear.

"I do not understand, Grandfather." Apistanewj rubs his ear and looks hurtfully at his grandfather, his eyes downcast. "How have I angered you? I am only following in the Prophet Wovoka. I only want peace. I only want an end to disease and old age."

Michaa Odjig snorts derisively.

This only emboldens Apistanewj, and he hardens his voice: "We can bring the living world and the spirit world together,

25

Grandfather. The Prophet says that all tribes of the people will be united as brothers as it was in the long before time."

"I have heard the stories, my child. I taught you the stories when you still suckled at your mother's breast." Michaa Odjig grows more agitated as he speaks. "I suppose the knife and the bow and the dish and the cup will be found again as well, and we will all eat heartily and there will be an end to hunger and thirst as well as disease and old age?"

Apistanewj tries to respond, but Micha Odjig cuts him off.

"Who have you been talking to, my child? Who has filled your head with this nonsense? How do you know of the Prophet Wovoka who lives in the far west of the Waste Lands and never comes here?"

Apistanewj motions towards the man at the center of the dancing ring. It is the older man in the felt hat again. "Whiskey Jack told me of him in a dream. He came to me with Coyote and said that Wovoka would bring us final peace if we just listened to him."

Michaa Odjig laughs disbelievingly. "Coyote is not to be trusted, Apistanewj. You know this. Or did I teach another grandson the ways of the People?"

"Mother listened to him, and she does not seem to have suffered for it."

"That remains to be seen, boy." Michaa Odjig shakes his head and draws swirls in the dirt with his walking stick. "She breathes yet, so there is plenty of time for sorrow."

"Besides," Apistanewj continues, "I made both Coyote and Jack swear to tell me only things that were true."

"A blanket of lies," Michaa Odjig chuckles mirthlessly, "is often woven from threads of truth." He then looks his grandson in the eye and changes the subject "And what of the white man in this plan of yours, boy? You were to bring peace with the white man. It was what you were born for. Will this dance of yours unite him with us, too? I do not see Fighting Bear dancing among you, but I am old and my eyes grow dim."

It is Apistanewj's turn for his voice to grow cold. "Do not mention Fighting Bear. He is no Human Being. He is a coward who allows other birds to lay eggs in his nest. He shrinks from honor and has forgotten the ways of the People and now sits alone in his own filth and misery instead of taking back his pride. He will not even..." The young man stops himself and takes a breath. "The white man will be driven from these lands." He says through gritted teeth. "He will return to the east and leave these lands for the People and Human Beings to govern ourselves."

"I see Lakota in that ring," Michaa Odjig points his stick in the direction of the dancing circle. The man in the middle now is the younger leather clad man in war paint. "I know what they believe will happen to the white man, and it is not to be driven back to the morning lands."

"Then the white man here will die and the rest will stay where they are."

"And what if the white man has the cup? Hmm? Where is it written that only Human Beings can have the tools of Father Yucca?"

"If such is the case," Apistanewj smiles grimly at his grandfather, "Then we will find the cup when we destroy the white man's cities and take it. If he has it, he stole it, just as he steals everything he owns."

"This is madness, boy!" Michaa Odjig kicks his heel at the ground. "This is not the way I taught you!"

"It is the only way, Grandfather." Apistanewj rises to his feet and begins to walk back to the circle. "I was born to bring peace to The People, and I will! You will see when I end sickness and old age."

Michaa Odjig watches as his grandson rejoins the circle. He shudders as he sees the shadows playing across the center man. They distort his features, his face seems snouted, his ears improbably long. Even his legs seem bent wrong in the dancing firelight. Then the vision steadies, and he is a man in a felt hat again, raising his arms to the sky and joining the chant.

Nä'nisa'na, nä'nisa'na
All our people are going up,

27

Above to where the Father dwells,
Above to where our people live.
Nä'nisa'na, nä'nisa'na
There will be no more aging
There will be no more sickness
Above where our people live.
The Father tells us so.

Michaa Odjig plants his stick firmly in the ground and pulls himself up. He turns away from the dancing men and women and moves in the direction home.

"The only way to end to end sickness and old age, boy," he mutters to his absent grandson, "is to die."

VII.

"Human Beings have never learned from their mistakes."
Ałk'idáá shook her head and continued spinning.

"And so they will ever be the fools of Father Yucca's
creation." Náásgóó said continuing to sew Kut's fabric into the
shawl.

"Can nothing be done, then?" Kut asked. "Is there no way of
saving the Human Beings from themselves?"

"It will be slow," the old woman said.

"Human beings have always grown like stones." The young
woman added.

"True," Kut agreed. "It always starts with one or two Human
Beings at a time. Change is slow, but when it comes it comes like
a mountain river when the snows melt."

"This all happened before," Ałk'idáá said again.

"And it will happen again," Náásgóó added.

"This time it is different." Kut said. "I feel it in my fingers. I
see it in the fabric, and I hear it on the wind."

"Perhaps," Náásgóó looked up and in doing so, pricked her
finger with the sewing needle. A drop of blood formed then
dropped onto the shawl.

Departure

For through long days of summer
I rambled through their orchards
And oakwoods all green
With the dew on the leaf;
And now that I have lost them
And lonesome among strangers
I sleep among the bushes
Or mountain caves alone,

-"John O'Dwyer of the Glen"
(traditional Irish ballad)

The seas may row, the winds may blow,
And swathe me round in danger,
My native land I must forego,
And roam a lonely stranger.
-"The Highlander's Farewell"
(traditional Scottish ballad)

It takes a thousand voices to tell a single story.
- Native American Adage

Chapter One
Percy

I.

I never knowed my Pa. He run off about three months before I was born. He went off to fight the Indians with Ardiss Drake, him that was the bastard son of Old Luther (but wouldn't nobody but a fool call Ardiss that to his face, not unless they was just fed up with life and lacked the sand to pull the trigger their own self).

"Some Pawnee chief's probably carrying your Pa's scalp on his belt right now," Ma'd say, then spit into the fire if we was in the cabin or on the ground if we wasn't. "Serve him right," she'd continue. "Least it's just his hair gets to trample all over hell's half acre now instead of the rest of his body." Then she'd look out towards the little graveyard we had behind the cabin. Gramps was out there, too, but I always knowed she was thinking of the other one. "I finally got that rat bastard to stay around more 'n one or two weeks at a time, and he's just about as useful now as he was then."

After the War Between the States, long before I was ever even thought about, Ma'n Pa moved out West. "Texas ain't home," he used to tell Ma, "but it's got fewer Yankees than Georgia does now." They settled in West Texas, and Pa became one of Drake's Riders. So he spent most his time out to Bretton in Ardiss' saloon with the other Riders playing poker, drinking whiskey, and keeping the decent folk safe from Redskins, bandits, and tax collectors.

Ma and him used to live right in Bretton with the other townsfolk. Two doors down from Ardiss and right between Lancaster O'Loch on one side and Gary Wayne Orkney on t'othern. But after Pa got hisself scalped and kilt, she moved out there to the edge of the Waste Land on her Pappy's place, and that's where I got brung into this world.

It took damn near forever before Ma would even talk about Pa with me. As a young'un, whenever I'd ask, she'd pull me into her lap and rock in her chair.

"Percy," she'd say, "Your Pa was a very brave man, but he was also a fool, which maybe I'm repeating myself." Then she'd stroke my brow the way mothers all can do to make you sleepy and forgetful about what you asked. "You don't need to fret about him, son." She'd whisper and look out at our little graveyard, "He ain't going nowhere no more, and he'll always keep an eye on you." Then just as I'd drift off to sleep, "You ain't got no need now to leave your Ma. You just stay here."

And I did for fourteen years.

About two weeks after my fourteenth birthday, Ma had a visitor. He showed up riding the biggest, cleanest, whitest horse I ever seen. He looked about as tall as God up there in that saddle. He was wearing a spotless white suit with his pants legs pressed into the tops of a couple of tan boots that came almost all the way up his knees. He wore his ginger-colored hair long, past his shoulders, and his mustaches and beard were well groomed. Everything about him from his wide-brimmed white hat to his oiled leather boots shone like sunlight. When he turned into our little yard and tipped his hat to Ma, I caught a gleam in my eye reflected from his hip.

He wore a pair of pearl handled pistols slung low.

Ma caught her breath when she saw him and clutched at her breast.

"Percy," she whispered. "Get on now. Go play at the creek. Ma has business with this gentleman."

When I tried to ask who he was, she shushed me and gave me a gentle push towards the creek.

I spent the better part of the morning spearing fish in the creek. Before he died, Gramps used to take me out here and teach me how to do that.

"Tell you what, son," he used to say, "any damned moron can hook a worm and trick a fish." He'd hand me a stick he'd spent the morning whittling to a point. "But it takes a man of skill and perfection to gig one." Then he'd take his own stick, stride purposefully into the creek, and absolutely fail to stick anything but the muddy bed. After a few times, I was able to gig at least one or two fish each time, so Gramps just got to where he'd smoke his pipe on the river bank and criticize my technique. Since Gramps passed on to the Sweet By and By, though, I often come out here to gig fish on my own and miss him.

Today, though, all I could think on was the mysterious stranger what had come up, and why Ma wanted me gone so all-fired much. I was a little upset with her. I never could get no fish with my mind like that, so I had to take a breather for a while and set a spell.

I had never seen nobody looked that clean before in my whole life. Not even Gramps when he took his Saturday night bath. I wondered who he was over and over until I begun to get the idea that maybe he was my own Pa. I had it all figured out. That would explain why Ma was so thunderstruck by him. He hadn't never been kilt by no Indian. He'd escaped and had set off back East to lead them Pawnee away from his family. He'd stayed there all this time making his fortune, so's he could come back when the coast had cleared of Indians and fetch us back.

The more I thought about this, the better I liked it, and after a while, I knowed it was so. I rose up from my bank and strode out to the middle of the creek with my spear in hand. I wanted to show Pa how well I could fetch dinner, and damned if I didn't gig twelve fish that morning.

He was just stepping off our back stoop by the time I got back with the fish. He had his hat under his arm now, and he was looking back over his shoulder at Ma, who leaned against the doorway with a strange look in her eyes, kinda grateful and sad all at once. Her hair was down where it had been all bunned up before, but other than that there wasn't no change. When he passed me by, I held the fish up to him, but I couldn't get no kind of sound to come out of my throat. He smiled at me, and I realized his teeth was white, too. Then he rustled my hair so my scalp tingled. I offered him the fish again.

"Take 'em into your Ma, son," he said and motioned in her direction. "I reckon you all will eat well tonight." His breath smelled like jasmine.

Son, I thought, he called me Son. Then you all will eat well. He ain't stayin'.

I didn't mean to, but I kinda slumped back to Ma. She didn't pay me no mind nor scold me for being sulky and rude to our visitor. She just kinda pulled me to her side and absently stroked my hair, but her eyes never strayed from him.

"Be seein' you, Laney." The man said as he pulled himself into the saddle and tipped his hat to her before puttin' it on again. "I'll tell the boys you said hey." Then he flicked the reins and turned his horse around and was gone out of the yard like he hadn't never been there to begin with.

"Who was that, Ma?" I asked looking into her faraway eyes.

Ma's voice hitched a little when she tried to answer. "An angel, Son."

Then I knew Pa really was dead, and he wasn't never coming back, but I was glad to have got to see him this once.

During supper that night, Ma still didn't say nothing. She never was what you would call a big talker or a social butterfly, but that night it was worse. Ma had a way to look at a fella and have whole conversations without opening her mouth. She could look at you and you knowed she was there, like she was inside you and kicking around your secret thoughts, but not like a thief or nothing, more like a librarian setting everything in its place.

Tonight, though, she kept staring at me, but the feeling was all different. It was like she was the one with the secret thoughts, and I couldn't get in there and straighten 'em out. It was like she was there, but at the same time, she wasn't. I figured she was thinking on Pa, but since I never knowed him, I couldn't join her

32

in her thoughts. There was a river between us, and I couldn't swim it. We ate our fish in silence.

If I coulda knowed something about Pa, I felt like we coulda talked that night. But Ma hadn't never told me nothing about him except what I done told you, which as you know wasn't nothing of a much at all. I tossed and turned all night. I wanted to know about my Pa, but I knew now, that if Ma wasn't gonna talk about him after spending all midmorning with his angel, she wouldn't never talk. I'd have to find out about him on my own, but I didn't know where to start.

Then it hit all at a sudden, like a blaze of glory. If Ma wasn't gonna talk, Pa's saddle partners probably would. There ain't nothing a cowboy likes more'n to sit around telling stories about the old days, and I bet if I could find one or two of Drake's Riders, I could find out all I wanted and more about Pa.

And I knowed where to look, too.

Bretton was a good ways off and the sooner I started on foot, the quicker I'd be there. I wrapped my slingshot, some smooth tiny creek rocks, and a couple of leftover fish in my good winter coat, then I tied the arms of the coat onto the end of my spear and crawled out the bedroom window trying hard not to wake Ma in the next room.

I might as well have stomped around all I wanted and played the fiddle to boot, for all the good it did me to sneak. Ma was standing by Pa's grave when I slinked that away to hit the road from behind. I got ready for a hiding and began laying plans for setting out the next week.

"If you're set on going tonight, boy, you best take Lippy," she said as soon as I got up close to her. Lippy was our mule. He was about eight days older than God, but he was all we had to pull the plow.

"Ma'am?"

"If you're set on going, you'll never get there this side of forever just on your feet," I could see glistening streams on her cheeks in the moonlight. "Take Lippy."

"How you gonna plow without Lippy?" I asked setting my pack down next to Gramps' wooden cross.

"I reckon I got along just fine before I had you to look out for me," Ma looked down at Pa's marker. I figured she couldn't bear the sight of me all packed up to go. "I reckon I got along fine without that mule, too. Take Lippy before I change my mind, boy."

"Yes'm." I turned towards our stable.

"I didn't keep your Pa's saddle when they brung him back," Ma said quietly. "I didn't plan on needing it, so I told Lank to keep it or burn it or throw it away for all of me." She paused as if so much talking all at once had wore her out. "I'll go fetch you a quilt to throw on Lippy's back. It ain't much, but it'll do."

"Yes'm."

I went on into Lippy's stable when Ma didn't say nothing else and turned for the house. I fixed up a harness for the spear and found an old canvas bag I could stow my gear in and sling over Lippy's rump. By this time Ma had brung in the quilt. She showed me how to fold it into a make-do saddle so I wouldn't get so rump-sore on the trail.

When this was finished, I turned to her to tell her bye and make promises to come back that even then I knew would have been lies, but she stopped me.

"If you're hungry, and there ain't no fish to be caught or game to kill, steal what you need to live, food or money, but ask forgiveness at the next church you pass."

"Yes'm." I opened my mouth again to make the empty promise, but she cut me off again.

"If you see a lady or a child in need, you got to help'em. Ain't nobody but fools nowadays to look after womenfolk and their young'uns."

"Yes'm." I opened my mouth again, but she grabbed me around the shoulders and shut me up a third time.

"If you see anything you don't understand while you're out there," she said, "don't be asking foolish questions. You won't like the answer none too much like as not. It's a good way to get yourself shot asking the wrong questions at the wrong time."

I knowed better by this time to try to get a word in edgewise, so I just kept my mouth shut and waited for her to continue.

"You better get. Don't say another word, or I can't bear to let you go." Then she pulled me to her again, and I squeezed her little body tight (I hadn't ever realized how little she was). She put her arms around me and squeezed, too, but it didn't have no real strength behind it, like hugging a corpse.

Then I mounted Lippy, kicked his shanks and we ambled out the stable and through the gate. Ma wasn't nowhere to be seen when I turned back to wave one last time.

II.

I wandered days and camped nights. I had to camp under the open sky on account of I didn't think to bring no tent or nothing. The Waste Lands get awful cold at night, and all I had was the quilt Ma give me, and while it could get pretty toasty on a winter night in a cabin and helped by a fire, it provided little comfort under the stars without even a campfire to help. Gramps had tried to teach me about setting fires like the Indians, knocking rocks together or rubbing catgut and twigs, but none of it ever took with me. I never really figured on needing it back then, but lying on the cold ground at night with only a quilt for comfort, I sure wished I'd a listened to him. Eventually, though, I discovered that if I could wrap the quilt around me and find a place to lay with my back protected and get Lippy to settle down in front of me, I could keep fairly warm at night, or at least not freeze to death.

I reckon Lippy and me traveled about three days before we ever caught on that I had done got lost somewhere. I remember one morning when I was overcome with curiosity about Pa and his days with Ardiss, I asked Gramps whereabouts Bretton was, and he said it was quite a bit east of our homestead, and I asked him which away east was, and he pointed at the sun.

"Thataway," he said. "The sun's east of here now."

Well, I'm sure you can see what my problem was. I had lit out at night when the sun wasn't nowhere. I had always figured on getting out a ways from home and sleeping under the stars. I figured that way the sun would wake me up in the morning, and I'd follow it. And that's just what I did, but I must of fallen asleep on the wrong side of the sun because I'd follow the sucker all day and it seemed like I'd wind up just about where I started again.

After three days of camping in the same site, I figured it was time for me to do something different. I rose up in the morning and went the opposite way of the sun. Every time I stopped for vittles' or a nap or to relieve myself, I'd check the sun and go off in the other direction. The scenery was different at least, but I be damned if I still didn't wind up right where I had set off from that morning or near enough as to make no difference.

It must of been some Indian sorcerer or something had put a spell on me. It was the only thing what made sense. I bet I'd done tramped all in some redskin's holy land or burial ground that night when I'd left Ma's and a medicine man or something had fixed it so's I'd get turned around and wander the Waste Land for the rest of forever. Yeah, I bet that the sun wasn't even where I saw it. The Indians can do stuff like that. Well, I may of fell off the covered wagon, but it wasn't yesterday I done it. If it looked like the sun was in one place, in front of me, say, it must really be catty-cornered to there. All I had to do then was put the sun on my side and walk that away.

So that's just what I done. When I woke up the next morning, I took a bearing on where the sun was, turned right, and set off. By mid-afternoon or so, I noticed the sun had moved clear over to my other shoulder. I knowed then that there really was some kind of Indian witchcraft afoot, and I done outsmarted 'em. I kept on moving, paying the sun no mind. I was finally on my way.

The first few days of wandering, I felt like I was really making headway. I hadn't seen the same scenery over and over, so I figured I was well on the way to Bretton. But the farther I got with no Bretton in sight, the more I began to miss the familiar scenery of a few days ago. I wasn't where I wanted to be, sure, but at least I knew where I was.

As the days wore on, food got scarcer, and it got harder and harder to find water, too. I only passed one cabin in all my rambling around that country, but when I went up to it, wasn't nobody there. The door was wide open, though, so I took that as a sign to come on in. It was dark inside, darker than it had any right to be so close to the middle of the day, and I hollered for whoever lived there, but didn't nobody answer. I moved a little bit further in when my nose caught a scent from the back.

Whoever lived here must of left pretty quick because there was near bouts a whole skillet of bacon on the cook stove. Well, I just stood there a minute and looked at it, taking in that sweet hickory smell and savoring, for just a minute the way it made my belly squeeze up just a little in anticipation. I remembered Ma tellin' me to steal what I needed on the road, so I started to reach out for the bacon and stow it in my haversack, but my conscience started bothering me something awful. It didn't seem right, Ma tellin' me to steal when she'd done gone to all the trouble of teaching me my Bible and the Ten Commandments, and my hand froze just over the greasy slab cooling in the pan.

But then I remembered her also telling me not to question things didn't make no sense to me, so I grabbed the bacon, shoved in my canvas bag, and left the cabin.

It had gotten so I couldn't ride Lippy no more on account of his getting so thin and weak, and he wouldn't have nothing to do with the bacon. I wished I had thought to grab some oats or something from the cabin, but I couldn't turn around and go back in that cabin again. It was just too creepy. I had to just lead him, and that slowed us down even more. I started to wish I hadn't ever started on this trip, and I couldn't understand how Ma could just let me go like she did without even trying to keep me there. I had a good mind to turn right around and go back and tell her so to her face. Except I didn't know which direction to go to get back any more than I knew which direction to go to town. I was in a fix sure enough. Following the sun, either way hadn't helped me, going against the sun hadn't done no better, and wandering whichever way my intuition told me to wasn't no good either.

Then Gramps showed up for breakfast one morning and set me straight.

III.

I woke up to the smell of bacon, and that didn't strike me as strange. My feet were unusually warm for the morning, too, because they was right up next to the fire, and that didn't strike me a strange neither. I could hear the bacon sizzling in the pan and the sound of a fork turning it every minute or so, again, not strange to me at all. What was strange, though, strange enough for me to sit up and take all the rest of this in, was the sound of my grandfather's hacking cough?

Now that's weird, I thought. You'd figure being dead, he'd not have that cough no more.

"Well, boy," Gramps eyed me from under the brim of his slouch hat and waved his cooking fork in my direction. "It ain't quite noon yet, you sure you wanna be getting up this early?"

"I thought you was dead." I rubbed the sleep out of my eyes and stood up, stretching my back.

"See there?" he plopped two strips of bacon on a plate and handed to me. "I always said you wasn't half the fool folks take you for."

I took the plate and began eating my breakfast. Gramps poured me some coffee from the percolator on the fire.

"Well, thank you," I said and took a sip. I never did care for the stuff, but I figured it'd be impolite of me to refuse the old man since he'd come so far. I was a little surprised to find that this cup tasted pretty good. Like drinking a campfire.

We sat there in silence for a bit while I ate my breakfast. After I finished the first few strips of bacon, Gramps plopped the rest on my plate.

"You gonna eat any?" I asked.

"What the hell I need to eat for?" Gramps asked as he began rubbing sand into the frying pan.

I shrugged and finished the plate.

"So that's it?" Gramps sounded kind of put out. "That's the biggest question you got for me? Am I gonna eat?"

I just looked at him while I took another sip of coffee.

"You ain't even a little curious about what I'm doing here? I only been dead for the last two years."

I kind of shrugged my shoulders. "Mama told me not to be asking questions about things I didn't understand. She said it was a good way to get myself in trouble."

"Smart woman."

"Besides, I figured if you wanted me to know what you was here for, you'd let me know soon enough."

Gramps reached into his shirt pocket and pulled out his pipe. From the hip pocket of his jeans, he took his tobacco pouch, and he began packing the pipe, tamping the tobacco down with his thumb. When he finished that, he pulled an ember out of the fire, held it to the bowl and sucked on the stem until the pipe lit. He took a few satisfied tugs before handing me the pipe. I shook my head and took another sip of coffee.

"Your mother's a smart girl," Gramps said, "and ordinarily I wouldn't think of contradicting any advice she gave, but you're gonna need to ask a question or two before it's all over. Pay attention to the folks around you, and you'll know when it's okay to ask questions."

"Yessir."

"You lost ain't you?"

"Yessir."

"How'd you get here?"

"I don't rightly know," I explained. "First, I went one way, then I went another. Next, I went whichever way seemed to suit me, and I wound up here. Wherever here is." I waved a hand to take in all the scenery.

"Well, it's all that wandering that got you in this fix, boy," Gramps chuckled. "What you want is to sit still for a bit and let the world come to you. It's the first rule of being lost: sit your ass still so folks can find their way to you."

"Ain't nobody looking for me," I reasoned. "How they gonna find me?"

"You weren't looking for me, but you found me easily enough."

Well, I couldn't argue with that, so I just finished the last of my coffee. Gramps stood up, patted the dust off his legs, and considered the campfire a bit. He stared at the smoke rising off it and followed it all the way to the sky.

"Too white," he muttered, gathered up some brush, and threw it on the flames. The flames died down a bit, but the smoke turned dark. "Better," he nodded then looked at me.

"Why'd you…" I started to ask, but then I realized he wasn't nowhere. The cook stuff was all gone, my tin cup, too. The only things left was Gramps' flint and tinder box and a little hatchet lying next to the smoldering fire and the black smoke rising lazily into the morning sky.

Chapter Two
Gary Wayne & Boris

I.

Two men dressed in denim and chambray, one hunched on his heels, the other reclining against a boulder with a black slouch hat pulled over his eyes, contemplated the coals of their own smoldering campfire as the first sipped coffee out of a tin cup. After a few minutes of silence, he set his cup on a nearby rock, rose off his heels, and raising his hands over his head and facing the rising sun, stretched his back until he was almost doubled backward. As he returned to a more natural posture, he ran a hand through his ginger hair, yawned loudly, and released a long and satisfying fart.

"We will get him today," he affirmed as if answering an unasked question from his partner.

His partner merely raised the brim of his hat enough to peer at him and wrinkled his nose with a snort, whether in response to his friend's assertion or for more aromatic reasons was unclear. His companion clearly assumed the former.

"We will, Boris. The bastard can't run forever. A fellow can't do what he done and expect to get away Scott-free."

Boris did not overtly respond to this. He merely rose from his position, dusted his pants legs off, and began to clean up the campsite.

"We've chased the son of a bitch across this damned desert for days. We have to be getting closer to him."

Boris shrugged and took a final pull from his coffee cup before pouring the dregs from both cups over the coals. He walked to edge of their campsite and put a handful of desert sand into both cups. He pulled a black and red checked bandana from his hip pocket, wrapped it around his hand before rubbing the grit into each cup in turn.

His companion seemed oblivious to his silence, talking on as if engaged in an in-depth conversation with himself.

"He hasn't even tried to cover his back trail that much. I mean it's like he wants to get caught. Probably a guilty conscience. I reckon a murdering traitor can feel guilt just like regular folks. Don't seem natural, but I guess it's possible. We'll catch him alright, it ain't nothing but God's own will that we do. Justice will prevail. I trust that it's so."

"Pfft," Boris spat at the ground as if he were spitting on the devil's own face. "Justice," he muttered with a grin that was more sneer than smile, "Jesus wept on the cross, Gary Wayne. Get a grip on yourself before you start sounding like Merle."

"What the hell's that supposed to mean?" Gary Wayne looked incredulously at Boris and fought the urge to cross himself against his friend's blasphemy. "You don't think we oughta be chasing after him?"

"I believe," Boris said slowly as to a small child struggling to understand a difficult scripture, "that we are acting according to the wishes of our sheriff and friend. Justice has nothing to do with it."

"So you don't think the bastard needs to hang."

"What I think and what we are doing are two entirely different things. I think if Ardiss'd wanted Lank brought to 'justice,' he'd a sent us out when it first happened and not let the poncey son of bitch get more than a day's lead on us."

Gary Wayne turned on Boris, his mouth agape in astonishment. "You think it's all a sham." He accused. "I suppose next you'll tell me that Ardiss encouraged the rat bastard to take liberties with his wife."

"If Lank'd taken the liberties with his wife, we'd never had to be out here in the first place," Boris muttered.

"Ardiss's wife, shitwit. You know what I meant." Gary Wayne turned back to the fire pit and began furiously kicking sand over the coals, muttering to himself. Boris continued packing their gear into saddle bags, shaking his head and smiling grimly at his partner's unfocused wrath.

II.

Gary Wayne Orkney had always let his guts get the better of his common sense. When he was seventeen years old, he became the youngest of Drake's Riders. His mother, it's true, was Ardiss Drake's half-sister, but this happenstance of nature had little to do with his appointment. Gary Wayne's parentage might have been enough to get him an audience with the regal sheriff, but if so, it could do that and no more. While Ardiss believed fully in the thickness of his blood, he saw duty and justice as rock solid: neither blood nor water could alter or influence it.

Before setting out on his journey to Bretton, Gary Wayne's father had counseled his son to be patient.

"If you're set on this path, boy," Elliott Orkney glared at his son from the head of the dinner table and tried to look fatherly and wise as he spoke around a shank of mutton and accented each word by pointing the business end of his fork in Gary Wayne's general direction, "wait for your moment like a cat waits on a mouse. Con your vantage, and make yourself indispensable without actually putting yourself into real danger. After all, you'll be more useful to Ardiss alive than dead, will you not?"

Elliott Orkney had himself been unable to ride with Ardiss due to an unspecified wound received as youth during the War of Northern Aggression. While few had ever actually seen this wound, few doubted his words. Indeed until the arrival of Reverend Merle Tallison, Elliott Orkney had been considered by many to be Ardiss Drake's chief advisor and de facto member of Drake's Inner Circle.

For once, Gary Wayne stood quietly, allowing his father to finish his parting advice. When the old man paused long enough to spear another bit of mutton with his fork and shove it into his mouth, Gary Wayne bowed slightly, taking his leave. "I thank you for the advice, Father," he said turning to go, then over his shoulder, "I'll telegraph when I get there."

He never did.

It was All Saint's Day when he arrived in Bretton, and the town had gathered in the Commons for the midday meal. Gary Wayne spied Ardiss on a dais at one end of the field, his wife, Guernica, to his left and Rev. Tallison to his right asking grace, and he made straight for the sheriff. As he drew within ten feet of Drake, he found his way blocked by a tall and slender man, of about forty.

"And where you think you're going, cully?" the man said from beneath a gray and tobacco stained Walrus mustache. Gary Wayne found himself eye-level with the tin star on his leather vest.

"I'm here to see Ardiss," Gary Wayne replied with, to his credit, only a hint of irritation.

"Well, then, you must be the Son o'God himself then, to be prancing up here like you own the place."

"I aim to see Ardiss," Gary Wayne repeated.

"You can see Mister Drake just fine from you are, Sonny," the man reached out to Gary Wayne's shoulder, probably to turn him about and maybe to help him find a seat amongst the townspeople, but this was too much for Gary Wayne, who delivered a quick jab to the taller man's kidney before he could touch him.

"I aim to see Ardiss," Gary Wayne repeated, this time, loud enough to draw the attention of those nearby.

The older man doubled over for only a second, and when he rose again, it was with his pistol drawn and aimed directly at Gary Wayne's temple. "You little puke," he screamed, surprisingly loud given his injury, "They'll be cleaning your worthless shit brains outta the trees for a week!"

Before things could progress much further, though, a weather-beaten hand reached from behind the gunman and forced his gun arm down.

"Who's our guest, Caleb?" While the voice was subdued and even, there was no question of its authority. The man behind Caleb, though clearly in his mid-thirties, seemed the elder of the two with his sleepy eyes, graying hair, and full beard.

His voice seemed to take the wind right out of Caleb, who re-holstered his gun with a sigh. "I got no idea, Ardiss. He just come up here, pretty as you please and demanded to see you. When I tried to find him a place at the table here, the son-uva-bitch gut-punched me." Caleb raised his shirt and pointed at his kidney as if to prove his story.

Ardiss swung his attention to the newcomer. "Well, is that a fact?" Ardiss chuckled a little and patted Caleb on the shoulder. "And who might you be, Little Cockspur?"

"My name is Gary Wayne Orkney, Sir," Gary Wayne stood straight and nervously brushed imaginary dirt from his shirt front, "and I'm here to join your Riders."

Caleb let out a guffaw, then immediately doubled over again. "That's rich," he wheezed through clenched teeth, "and him twelve years old and never killed more'n a squirrel, I reckon."

"Peace, Caleb," Ardiss waved Caleb away, "Go fix your plate." Then turning again to the younger man. "Orkney, huh? You Margie's boy?"

"Yessir."

"Well, you coulda said so to begin with and spared my deputy the bruised kidney. My kin is welcome to break bread with me, especially on a holiday, but I'm afraid Caleb's right. I can't deputize just anybody for the asking. You ever done any hard riding, son?"

"I rode two weeks all the way here." Gary Wayne couldn't help throwing his chest out a little. "I reckon that was pretty hard ridin'."

Ardiss smiled and shook his head gently. "Polishing your pants on saddle leather for two weeks don't make you a Rider, son. There's a whole lot more to it than sitting in the saddle and lettin' your feet hang down. Now you're blood kin, and I'm glad to have you in my home here. You're welcome to stay as long as you want, but kin don't mean nothing when it comes to the Law. A man ain't born a Rider; he becomes one. Do you understand what I'm saying to you, son?"

"You're telling me I can't be a Rider until I prove myself."

"That's right, son. Now let's see if we can't get you set up for some food here, and we'll get you situated in the house after dinner."

Ardiss guided Gary Wayne by the shoulder, and this time, Gary Wayne allowed himself to be touched, though he did bristle a bit at first. They moved through the crowd until they came to Caleb, who was still rubbing his abdomen and glaring at Gary Wayne.

"Caleb," Ardiss said, patting his deputy on the back with his free hand, "I want you to help my nephew here find himself a place at the table, preferably up with the family, and show him where to fix his plate. Gary Wayne's going to be staying with us for a little bit, and I want him to feel welcome."

Caleb said nothing, just mumbled under his breath and continued to stare at Gary Wayne.

"Do we have a problem, Caleb?" Ardiss's voice dropped just a little bit. Gary Wayne looked like he was preparing to have to punch another kidney.

"No, Ardiss," Caleb claimed, "we ain't got a problem."

"That's good. It don't take a very big man to carry a grudge, and I'd like to think I'm a better judge of character than that." Ardiss turned to go, walked a step or two away, and, as if in afterthought, turned back to face his nephew.

"Gary Wayne?" he asked.

"Yes, sir?"

"You serious about joining us?"

"Yes, sir. Dead serious."

"Good. Then you listen close to everything Caleb tells you. In addition to being my lead deputy, Caleb is also my city manager. And you are his new stable boy."

With that Ardiss turned and rejoined his wife, who was already eating and in deep discussion with a tall man all in white to her left.

III.

By Christmas, Gary Wayne had suitably impressed Caleb enough to be promoted from swabbing muck from the horse stables to cleaning the City Hall and serving the Sheriff and his guest during official dinners. This promotion was in no small way due to the calming influence of Boris McAllister, one of Caleb's other apprentices and the son of one of Ardiss' business partners. Boris was a large, quiet boy. He would rarely answer a question directly or immediately. Instead, Boris would stare blankly at his interrogator, often for as long as minute, before tendering his answer. It was for this reason that most of the townspeople considered him "a little slow" or "not right bright."

Gary Wayne was no different when he met him. It was his first day in the stables, and he was pleasantly surprised to find that he was going to have company during his purgatory amongst the horse droppings.

"Well, hey there, partner," Gary Wayne boomed as he took off his duster and hung it on a peg. "Name's Gary Wayne. How you doing this fine morning?" Gary Wayne walked towards Boris with his hand outstretched, grinning from ear to ear.

Boris stared blankly at Gary Wayne, tongue running slowly between his teeth and lips. As Gary Wayne waited his hand slowly sank by degrees to his side. After almost a minute, Gary Wayne began to turn his attention to the shovel in the corner, which apparently wasn't going to scoop the manure itself.

As Gary Wayne turned away from Boris and reached for the shovel, Boris sniffled and cleared his throat quietly. "I'm doing fairly well," he said in a quiet baritone. "I don't really have room to complain."

Gary Wayne began cleaning the nearest stall without response. *What's the point*, he wondered, *the fella's obviously touched.*

They worked side-by-side in silence for a week. Every once in a while, Gary Wayne would catch Boris watching him out of the side of his eyes, but Boris never said anything to him, so Gary Wayne returned the favor.

By the beginning of the second week, though, things began to change. Caleb, a man quick to wrath and slow to forgive, did everything he could to discourage Gary Wayne from pursuing an appointment to the Riders. As Ardiss' nephew, Caleb knew he couldn't really harm the boy, but he could make his life miserable enough to send the dumbass bastard packing. So while other boys his age were cleaning the firearms and learning the finer points of gunmanship from other Riders, Gary Wayne spent his days shoveling manure in the stables. Hell, Caleb even let Boris take a day off to go hunting with his father and Ardiss once.

"Why not?" Caleb responded when Boris asked him the evening before. "I'm sure Mr. Orkney there'd be more'n happy to cover for you in the stables tomorrow. Wouldn't you, boy?"

Gary stared blankly at Caleb as he pulled his jacket on to go home. "I reckon," he replied.

"So long as you'd be agreeable to do the same for him one of these days when I can spare him for a day off gallivanting."

Boris considered this for about two seconds. "I don't see where that would be much of a problem."

Gary Wayne turned his back to the two of them and moved toward the stable door. "Fat chance of that happening anyway," he muttered as he reached what he assumed would be the range of Caleb's hearing.

"What's that, boy?" Caleb called, hooking one hand behind his ear, "I didn't quite catch that. My kidney must be distracting me."

"I didn't say nothing, Caleb, not a word."

Boris took in this exchange silently, watching both men closely. Old Braddock, the negro stable master drew in a quick breath, shook his head, and slipped out back for a smoke.

Caleb's voice developed a slight growl, "That's Mister Ecton, to you, boy, and you did say something."

Well, I gave him an out, Gary Wayne thought, *not my fault if he didn't take it*. "I was just considering the likelihood of your ever giving me a chance to do anything in this town but swab shit, and I found them lacking, Sir Mister Caleb Ecton, Sir."

"I see your point," Caleb allowed. "Allow me to rephrase then." He turned his attention back to Boris. "I am sure, son, that in the highly unlikely event that I let Mr. Kidney, here, out of my sight, you'd be more than agreeable to cover for him in his absence."

Boris looked uncomfortably at Gary Wayne. Unable to find any suitable answer to this that didn't put Gary Wayne or Caleb in a bad spot, yet still allowed him to go hunting the next morning.

Gary Wayne, however, came to his rescue. "Ain't no reason to answer that Boris. You're a man of honor, I can tell, and of course you'd help a fellow out if he needed it. Fact is, I'd be happy to help you out tomorrow and wouldn't even ask you to return the favor. No, I'm going to bid you gentlemen good night."

Boris quietly let out the breath he had been holding. Thanking the good Lord and all that was holy that Gary Wayne had taken the high road and controlled his temper.

Unfortunately, though, Caleb could not let the younger man have the last word. "You sure are a card, Gary Wayne," he laughed, "and you sure got the right job here in these stables. You're so full of shit, I can smell you from here."

Gary Wayne, who had just opened the stable door, stopped in his tracks, the cold autumn wind blowing in his face. When he slowly turned around again to Caleb, his face was as beet red. Boris suspected the wind had little to do with it.

He we go, he thought.

If he pushed it, Gary Wayne wouldn't stand much of a chance against Caleb this time. Caleb, Boris now understood, had orchestrated this whole scene to push the younger man to a fight, and he had timed it perfectly. It was late afternoon, and Gary Wayne usually worked so hard that by midday, his strength was waning. By now, he had to be doing good just to stand.

Boris watched Gary Wayne's fists clench and unclench, and turning, he could see Caleb set his feet firmly waiting for an attack.

An attack that never came.

Gary Wayne took a deep breath, pulled his jacket tighter around his chest and settled his shoulders more comfortably into it, chuckling coldly. "Smell me from there, huh," he chuckled again. "Well, that shouldn't be no problem for a genuine son of a bitch."

With that Gary Wayne turned and walked through the door, being sure to close it behind him.

Caleb just stared blankly at the door for minute, then he, too, started chuckling. "Son of a bitch, huh? That boy may be all right after all." He clapped Boris on the shoulder, nearly knocking the young man over. "Enjoy your day off, kid." Then he, too, pulled on his coat and left Boris alone in the stables staring blankly out the door into town square.

"Quit bucking him," Boris advised Gary Wayne two days later when he returned to the stables.

"Who?"

"Caleb. Quit bucking him if you want to move out of the stables." Boris told him what Caleb had said after Gary Wayne left.

"What does that have to do with anything? He's still a son of a bitch."

"Sure he is," Boris explained, "but he's your son of a bitch. Ardiss don't do nothing without he's got a purpose. He gave him to you for a reason."

"And what might that reason be, you think?"

Boris shrugged and refused to say anything else.

Great, Gary Wayne thought. *I broke him. He ain't used to saying so much in one sitting, and I used up all his allotment.*

"Impress Caleb," Boris responded two hours later, "and you impress Ardiss. Quit bucking."

"Okay," Gary Wayne raised his hands in surrender, "I'll quit bucking."

Three weeks later, Gary and Boris were moved to the kitchen, and by the middle of December, they were waiting tables, and on New Year's Day, Gary Wayne was deputized.

IV.

And now, just over ten years later, he and Boris found themselves riding almost a week into the desert, sleeping cold under the stars, drinking mud passing for coffee, and hunting a man they had ridden with, fought beside, and considered all but blood-kin.

"Bastard couldn't keep his dick in his pants, plain and simple," Gary Wayne spoke to the air as if answering a question anybody would know the answer to. Boris hadn't spoken a word for at least half an hour, since busting camp and remounting the hunt. "All them doxies across the way and he's got to prod the boss's woman. It's just damned inconsiderate if you ask me."

"Indeed," Boris said quietly, riding beside his friend with the morning sun at their backs, "and that's why we're chasing the bastard all of Hell's Waste because he was inconsiderate."

"I don't know about you," Gary Wayne gave his friend a hard stare, "but I'm chasing the bastard because he killed half a dozen sworn deputies, including my baby brother, in the process of performing their legal and ethical duty, while he tried to escape justice."

Boris let this pass without comment, and the two rode on in silence. Boris had to admit that the man had a point. Lancaster O'Loch had betrayed his sheriff, but more importantly, he had betrayed his friend. He and Ardiss had ridden together longer than anyone. They had met shortly after Ardiss became sheriff. Boris remembered the story well, having heard some version of it from one or the other of them for what seemed the whole of his adult life. Let the whiskey flow long enough, and Ardiss or Lank would pull out that old chestnut and chew on it all night.

Ardiss was barely twenty then, full of sap and very green. Being the youngest sheriff in the history of Bretton, he never let a chance to prove his sand and reinforce his authority slip by. Any minor infraction of the law, custom, or common decency, from spitting to public drunkenness, would find the offender not only punished to fullest extent of the law but also the recipient of an outraged tongue-lashing by the "boy-king," as the local wags took to calling him.

About a month or so after he took office, Ardiss was out riding the range when he came upon another rider approaching him on the narrow trail. The stranger couldn't have been much older than Ardiss, but he rode his horse with an authority that implied a dignity beyond his years. He was clad head to toe in white: white, flat-brimmed Stetson, white linen suit (albeit with a gray string tie), and the palest tan riding boots Ardiss had ever seen. His ginger hair was long, almost to his shoulders, and he wore his mustaches below his chin and waxed to perfection.

Ardiss pulled his horse off to the side in order to let the stranger pass and nodded as he rode by. The stranger did nothing in return as he passed, didn't even look in Ardiss' direction.

"Howdy," Ardiss said, nodding his head again.

The stranger said nothing.

By this time, Ardiss was mad enough to bite himself, but he tried his best to maintain his calm. "Perhaps you're new to these parts," he said slowly and crisply, "and don't know we got manners out here."

"Oh," the stranger absently waved his hand, his back to Ardiss as he moved further down the trail, "Howdy."

This nonchalance made Ardiss even angrier if such a thing were possible. He reined his horse around and moved after the insolent newcomer. "Hey," he called, "That ain't good enough, sir."

The stranger pulled his horse to a stop and slowly turned his mount around to see the young sheriff approach him, but he said nothing.

"You hear me, boy?" Ardiss' face was reddening steadily as the stranger's silence persisted. "I ain't a man to be disrespected."

At this, the stranger chuckled. "Indeed, you're barely a man at all," his voice was as smooth as fine silk. "There can't be more than two winter's difference between us."

This was too much for Ardiss, who stopped his horse and drew one of the .36 caliber Colt Navy revolvers he'd so recently inherited from his father. "Get off your horse, and say that to my face, you silver-tongued sonuvabitch."

The stranger smiled again from his seat but made no effort to dismount. "You're going to shoot me, sir? Bad manners is a capital offense here, is it?"

"A lot of things are killing offenses in the Waste Lands," Ardiss replied, "Disrespecting the duly-appointed law, for one."

The stranger nodded thoughtfully, "I see," he responded. He had an accent that Ardiss couldn't quite place, "and neglecting to make my manners to young men on the trail constitutes disrespecting the law, does it?"

"It does if the young man is the local sheriff."

"Ah, and you are, I take it, the local sheriff?" The stranger swung his leg up over his horse and climbed out of the saddle. "My mistake. Please accept my sincerest apologies, Mr...?"

"Drake, Sheriff Ardiss Drake," Ardiss did not lower his gun or make a move to dismount, "and you ain't getting out of it that easy."

"No sir, *Sheriff* Drake," The stranger smiled, and Ardiss couldn't quite tell if it was at his expense, "the merest thought hadn't begun to speculate about forming in my mind, I assure you. However, being as we're apparently about to kill each other, it seems only fitting for me to introduce myself."

Ardiss did nothing, just stared impassively at him with gun raised.

"My name is Lancaster O'Loch late of Ireland and, more recently, New York. It would have been a pleasure to meet you." Lancaster approached Ardiss' horse with his hand outstretched and a grin on his face. Ardiss waved him away with the barrel of his gun.

"Back away and let me get down," Ardiss said. Lancaster stepped back.

"Oh, by all means, good sir," he said, stepping back, "but I must tell you, you're in danger of making a big mistake."

"Am I?" Ardiss holstered his gun and shifted his weight to dismount. "How's that then?"

Lancaster opened his coat and gestured at his waist. "You have me at a disadvantage, you see."

"You don't have any guns?" Ardiss asked in disbelief as he climbed off his horse and redrew his own iron.

Lancaster removed his jacket, folding it carefully over his saddle. "Well, sir, to tell you God's truth, I didn't really plan on needing them when I woke this morning, not knowing about your fanatical insistence on frontier courtesy." As he talked, Lancaster removed the cufflinks from his shirt sleeves and placed them in his trouser pockets. "I do have one or two counter-proposals for you if you're amenable." He began rolling up his sleeves. "We could indeed have a duel to the very death if that is the only way to satisfy your honor, but it seems to me to be a waste of good lead, and a bit discourteous in its own right, unarmed and defenseless as I am." Ardiss said nothing. "Or you could simply accept my most sincere apology for any hurt I've done you and we both be on our way."

Ardiss merely glared back, agitatedly fingering the trigger of his gun.

"Not interested, huh? Well, truth be known, I didn't really expect you to be, but it couldn't hurt to offer. There is one other option I suppose we could try unless you just have your heart set on murdering an unarmed man." Lancaster untucked his shirt and began unbuttoning it. "We could just have ourselves a good, old-fashioned country brawl and be done with it. What do you say?"

Ardiss considered this a second, looking thoughtfully at Lancaster and chewing the inside of his cheek. "Fair enough," he said, reholstering his gun and unstrapping his holsters from his hip.

"You see," Lancaster moved closer to Ardiss as the sheriff turned to hang his holsters over his horse's back, "I could tell right away that you were basically a man of honor," As Ardiss turned back to his opponent, Lancaster let fly with a ferocious left hook that sent the sheriff sprawling face-first on the wet and muddy ground, "if a bit overly trusting."

Lancaster moved to where Ardiss sprawled with a mouthful of dirt and the wind knocked out of him. As Ardiss tried to push himself up onto all fours, Lancaster lifted his leg to deliver a solid kick into the sheriff's side. Ardiss caught this movement from the corner of his eye, however, and managed to side-sweep his own leg in a somewhat less than graceful arc but connecting with his attacker's one grounded leg and knocking him off-balance. As Lancaster went tumbling, Ardiss struggled to his feet, spitting gritty mud and sour grass as he rose, still trying to catch his breath. As the Irishman lay on his back sucking in his own deep breaths, Ardiss took a moment, hands on thighs to catch his wind, too, only to lose his balance and tumble onto his opponent where the two of them grappled each trying to gain the advantage over the other or, at least, land a solid punch.

"So you think," Ardiss wheezed as Lancaster shifted his weight violently to his right, toward the downhill side of the trail, "that you can just … waltz into my territory … insult me … and not answer for it?"

As Lancaster shifted his weight, he pulled Ardiss into a bear hug and flipped over, landing precariously on the downhill slope, but with the sheriff underneath him. "Hardly, waltzing, sir. Merely preoccupied." He released Ardiss from the hug, pushing himself up with his left hand pressing into Ardiss' chest. "It does seem to me, though," he observed raising his right hand up for a punch, "that you're making an awfully large show over noth--"

The rest of his thought was cut off by first a scream then an agonized sigh as Ardiss managed to get his mouth around Lancaster's wrist and bite down, then jerk his leg straight into Lancaster's crotch with a surge or renewed energy.

Lancaster rolled further down the hill, and Ardiss managed to pull himself onto all fours and scrambled after him, still coughing up mud and plant. A beetle flew from his mouth as he coughed.

The Irishman managed to pull himself up to his knees, red-faced and teary, hands gripping the earth as if to keep him from flying off into space. Ardiss rose to his feet as he neared him and held out his hand.

"Truce?"

Lancaster nodded. Ardiss leaned down to help the man up; Lancaster grabbed the sheriff's outstretched hand and pulled back as hard as he could, flipping Ardiss over Lancaster's shoulders and onto his back in the mud. The effort was too much for the Irishman, though, and he fell beside the sheriff with a thud.

The two men lay side by side exhausted. Ardiss, with a groan, rolled to his side facing his adversary, balled his fist, and tried unsuccessfully to knock Lancaster in the head. The punch landed inches away from its target with barely enough force to indent the mud. For his part, Lancaster tried to lift his own fist and barely raised it three inches before it fell with a dull thud back to the ground.

"I win," Ardiss said through wheezing breaths.

"Like hell you do." Lancaster coughed up mud and tried futilely to sit up. "I'm still up for another go."

Ardiss had only enough energy left to roll his eyes in Lancaster's direction. "A draw then?"

"Fair enough." Lancaster managed on his second try to sit up, and he used his little finger to excavate mud from his inner ear. He looked down and his legs with a despondent sigh. "Ruined a perfectly good pair of trousers. Did you have to land in a puddle?"

"Think about that next time you disrespect someone on the trail." Ardiss, too, managed to struggle up to a sitting position. After working something in the back of his mouth diligently with his tongue, he spit out what bore a striking resemblance to a bicuspid. "You owe me a tooth."

"You owe me a new pair of trousers."

"How about I give you a job instead?"

"Doing what?"

"Well, you're discourteous, obnoxious, and you don't fight fair. Sounds like a lawman to me, and I need a deputy."

Lancaster considered this, nodding thoughtfully to himself. "Fair enough, boss. I'm your man."

While Boris daydreamed, Gary Wayne had pulled ahead and begun scouting the horizon, looking, one presumed, for tell-tale signs of Lank's passing. Boris' reverie was interrupted when Gary Wayne suddenly pulled his horse to a stop forcing Boris' mount to stop as well.

"Boris!" Gary Wayne was trying to both whisper and speak loudly enough for his companion to hear him. "Boris, look over there." He pointed to the horizon ahead of them and to the right. Boris could see immediately what had caught his friend's attention.

Wafting lazily up into the late morning sky was a thick cloud of black smoke. If he tried very hard, Boris could also just catch the scent of a wood-fire on the breeze coming from that direction.

Gary Wayne grinned at Boris with an uncomfortable gleam in his eye. "We got the murdering traitor now," he said, "Dumbass sunuvabitch. We got him now."

Chapter Three
Percy

I.

It was getting up to noon by the time Gramps had finished fixin' me breakfast and threw that brush on the fire. I figured ordinarily, I should be getting Lippy up and moving him along, but my traveling plans hadn't exactly worked out so good for me, and Gramps had said for me to sit tight, so I thought I'd give that a whirl. I reckoned when dead folks give advice, they probably got a reason for it. Besides, Lippy didn't look like he was feeling all that up to doing much walking today. He was breathing kinda heavy, and his eyes was all wide and startled.

I felt kinda bad for him after I had had such a good breakfast. I had waited on Lippy like one hog waits on another. I wished I hadn't set up all the bacon I stole from that cabin; Lippy looked about hungry enough now to eat jest about anything I put in front of him. I stood up to move over to him and kinda pet him up when I saw Lippy's oat sack laying on its side next to the campfire. Looked like oats was spilling out of it just a little, but they was the biggest damn oats I ever seen. One of 'em looked like it would just fit in the palm of my hand.

I grabbed the bag and brung it over to Lippy. He looked at me sickly, his eyes rimmed with water and dripping. He tried to lift his head up, but it didn't do no good. He could only ever get it a few inches off the ground before he had to lay it back down and try again.

"It's okay, boy," I told him squatting down on my haunches and hooking the bag behind his ears, "I'll bring it to you instead."

I swear Lippy smiled at me when I put the feedbag on him, and he seemed to feel better as soon as he took the first bite. I stayed right there while he ate, running my fingers through his short matted brown mane. He must have eaten nonstop for a good ten-fifteen minutes, but I couldn't tell that he'd even made a dent in the bag. He seemed strong enough to stand by now, though, and so I raised up off my haunches and give him a good tug on his leader rope, and he come up spry, like a newborn foal, and licked me right in the face.

Well, let me tell you, mule slobber ain't the kind of thing you want to let set on you none, so begun to look around for my blanket, spewing and spitting the whole way. When I saw it on the edge of the campsite all folded neatly and ready to throw over Lippy's back, I made for it, but I never did get a chance to use it. As I was bent over to pick it up, I heard a loud click behind me, and a man I ain't never heard before started yelling at me.

II.

"Drop it right there, you god-damned, sonuvabitching, wife-stealing, child-killing bastard!"

I didn't have nothing to drop; the blanket was still on the ground, so I just stood still.

"I said drop it!"

Then I heard another voice behind me, this one was a bit deeper and a whole lot calmer. "Gary," it said just like this was a conversation they'd done had three hundred times. "Simmer down."

"Don't tell me to simmer down," the first voice whined, "You lose a brother and then tell me to simmer down. I ain't simmering nothing!"

I was mighty afraid to move, but I figured if I was gonna get shot, I'd at least like to see who it was doing the shooting. I slowly turned my head so I could see behind me between my legs. Sure enough, there was two fellas behind me; one of them, the one with the gun drawn on me, had the reddest hair I had ever seen, and the other one was wearing a slouch hat that shaded most of his face; he just looked tired as all get-out, kinda leaning his weight all on one foot and sagging his shoulders.

Both of them wore stars on their blue shirts.

Well, I knowed then what this was all about.

"I can't drop it," I told them through my legs.

"Don't give me that horse shit, asshole," the redhead yelled. "Drop it now or I'll fill you so full of lead, you'll rattle when you walk."

I couldn't help it, I started crying a little, "Mister I can't drop it. Honest, I can't I done ate it all this morning. There ain't none left to drop."

Redhead lowered his gun just a little, and Slouch Hat sighed loudly. "Put that thing up, Gary, before someone gets hurt," Slouch that said. "This clearly ain't our man."

Redhead holstered his gun and said something under his breath what I couldn't make out. Slouch hat looked at me.

"Stand up straight and turn around son," he said, "I don't fancy spending all afternoon conversing with your backside."

I did as I was told and raised my hands to boot. "I'm sorry," I whimpered, "I was just hungry, and it was there on the stove. Wasn't nobody to ask, and Ma told me to take what I needed. I knowed it was wrong, but I ain't had time to ask Jesus about it yet. Please don't shoot me."

Slouch Hat looked like he was trying not to cough or vomit; his hand went to his mouth, and I could hear him gagging a little, but his eyes looked like he kinda enjoyed it. Redhead hit him in the arm and looked at me.

"Boy," he said irritably, "what the Sam Hell are you going on about? What did you eat?"

"I ate the bacon."

Slouch Hat snorted and coughed again, then turned away toward his horse.

Redhead ran his fingers through his hair. "You ate the bacon?"

"Yessir."

"What bacon?"

"The bacon I stole from the cabin." Redhead looked like he was choking on something; his face got all red, and it seemed like he couldn't breathe. By this time Slouch Hat had gotten himself under control, it looked like, and he came back over to where me and Redhead was talking.

"Gary Wayne," he said, "Let me handle this." He walked up to me and looked me right in the eye. Redhead turned his back on me and started examining the campsite. "We don't care about that bacon, son. What we want to know is if you've seen anyone else out here the last few days."

"Just my Gramps," I said with a sniffle.

"Can we speak with him, then?"

"I don't think so."

"Why not? Where is your grandfather?" Slouch hat started to look around the camp like Gramps might jump out from behind a tumbleweed or something.

"He's been dead for about five years," I explained as calmly as I could so as not to get Redhead all riled up again.

64

Wasn't no good, though. When I said this, Redhead spun around from where he was poking through the smoldering fire coals with a stick. "Weeping Jesus on the cross!" he hollered. "C'mon, Boris, this ain't getting us no damn where!"

Chapter Four
Gary Wayne & Boris

I.

This just damn typical, Gary Wayne thought as he poked through the red coals. *Not a soul on this trail for days on end. No sign of Lancaster, and when we finally do find somebody, I'll be burned if he's not feeble minded. Bacon! Jesus wept!*

He was only barely paying attention to Boris' interrogation of the boy. He feared if he was too involved, he might be overly tempted to put a bullet in either the kid's head or his own. Still, he had to admit that the kid clearly knew his way around a campfire. Gary Wayne could see that the fire had been prepared well: the ground cleared at least ten feet from the fire, and near perfect circle of rocks around the actual build to keep the fire from spreading.

Inside the circle, he could see that the boy had expertly built a fire for cooking. He could see the charred remains of two fairly thick logs set parallel to each other just far enough to support a skillet (Gary Wayne could even smell the bacon grease that had spattered onto the rocks and logs) and a coffee pot (Gary Wayne spied the coffee rings on the flattest of stones where the boy had apparently set his cup down to keep it warm as he went about his morning rituals). Maybe the boy wasn't as feeble-minded as Gary Wayne thought at first.

"Where's your grandfather?" he heard Boris ask the boy.

"He's been dead about five years," the boy said as calmly as saying he'd been reading and writing since he was six.

Or maybe not.

"Weeping Jesus on the cross!" Gary Wayne threw the stick he'd been using to poke through the fire coals into the fire pit, jumped up, and spun around in one fluid motion. "C'mon, Boris, this ain't getting us no damn where!"

As he stomped toward Boris and the boy, Gary Wayne ran the fingers of both hands agitatedly through his hair. *Lucky if it don't come out in clumps, he thought, the way this day's going.*

"Now look here, Boris," Gary Wayne stopped within two feet of his friend and set his feet firmly in a defensive stance. "We ain't got all Dad-blessed day to interview idiot-children. Every minute we waste here is daylight gone and Lancaster farther away."

Boris raised his hands placatingly. "I understand, Gary. Calm down before you give yourself a fit. I just want to ascertain that this boy didn't see anybody else pass this way."

"Anybody else besides his dead Pappy cooking breakfast, you mean?"

"Exactly."

"He wasn't my Pappy; my pappy's been dead…"

"You hush." Gary Wayne made a closing motion with his fingers.

"It was his granddaddy, Gary" Boris explained.

I'm an island O'Sane in a sea of crazy. Gary Wayne let out a long and frustrated sigh and waved his right hand in the boy's general direction emphasizing each word. "He spent the morning with his dead grandfather, Boris." The boy in question looked from one to the other, slowly nodding his head. "He ain't exactly the most reliable witness. He coulda seen eighteen Lancaster's leading an Army brass band, and it wouldn't amount to more than a fart in a whirlwind."

"I promise I ain't seen nobody else, Mister," the boy interrupted, "just…"

"Can it, kid." Gary Wayne motioned him away with a dismissive wave of his hand. "Boris, it ain't like Lancaster is easy to miss out here. Even if this kid ain't skull-fucking batshit, he's done told you he ain't seen nobody, and I'm fairly certain that nobody includes a ginger-haired Nancy in a pressed white suit. Now if you don't mind…"

"Well, now," the boy interjected, "I did see…"

Gary Wayne turned to face him with an icy glare. "Kid, I done told you twice now to hush. Don't make me tell you a third time. Now, Boris if you don't mind, I'd like to get a move on…"

"Yessir, But I did see," Gary Wayne glared again, and the flustered young man finished his thought in one word: "I-seen-that-fella-you-all-is-talkin'-about."

II.

Gary Wayne tried as best he could, but his voice absolutely failed to come. He just stood there staring gape-jawed.

Boris turned around like something had caught his attention and snickered a little. When he turned back, though, his face was all seriousness.

"You saw the man we're looking for?" Boris spoke slowly and calmly pausing between each word to make sure the boy understood what he was asked.

"Yessir," he replied. "The fella with the ginger hair and the white suit? I sure did."

This was, once again, too much for Gary Wayne, who did finally find his voice. "You just told us you hadn't seen nobody today!" he yelled.

"I said I'd seen my gramps!" the kid sounded defensive and hurt all at once.

"Besides him!"

Boris again tried to motion Gary Wayne to calm down, but he'd have none of it. "Goddammit, Boris, leave me be. This puke's been hiding something, and I aim to find out what!"

"I ain't lying, Mister!" the boy took a step towards Gary Wayne with such determination that the older man took a step back. "Now, I done some bad things the last few days, stealing bacon and such, but I ain't no liar, and I won't have nobody calling me one."

Boris turned to the younger man, contemplated calming him down, then he saw his expression. Something about the boy's face seemed familiar to Boris, but he couldn't take the time now to figure it out. He turned back to Gary Wayne, who seemed locked in a battle of sheer will with the kid. With a shrug, Boris moved out of the line of fire and took a seat on a rock, staring intently at the boy's face.

"I told you I ain't seen nobody this morning 'cept for Gramps, and that's the God's honest truth. I seen your fella three, four days ago."

"Where'd you see him then?" Gary Wayne's voice tried its best to sound stern and authoritative, but the best it could manage was a doubtful whine.

"Out at my ma's place. He come to see her a few mornings ago and left in the afternoon. I don't know where he was headed."

Gary Wayne stared at the boy as if he were judging his weight. From his seat on the rock, Boris cleared his throat. "Where's your ma's place, son?"

"Off that away I reckon." Percy waved one arm absently behind him. "I don't know," He balled his fists, hit the air beside his legs and cried in frustration. "I been lost ever since I left. Ain't seen nobody in all that time 'cept for Gramps and you, and when you two leave, I reckon I'll just wander all over until I die since I can't seem to get nowhere but here."

Gary Wayne simply stepped to the side and began studying the skyline in the direction the kid had indicated as if his mother's homestead might be just beyond the horizon. Boris stood from his perch and walked over to the whimpering boy. He bent over and put his arm across the young man's shoulders. "Where you trying to go, son?"

"Bretton." He looked into Boris' face and wiped one dust-covered fist across his eyes. It did little to improve his face, just smeared dirt into his tears and gave him a raccoon's mask. "I want to ask Ardiss Drake and his men about my pa on account of my ma don't like to talk about him. It just makes her sad."

"I can understand that," Boris reached into his hip pocket and removed a neatly folded red-and-black handkerchief. He handed it to the kid who smiled and began to rub as much of the trail of his face as he could. "Your dad was a good man, and your ma loved him very much. Shouldn't nobody have to bury their husband that early and raise a young'un on their own."

Gary Wayne, who seemed convinced now that Lancaster wasn't going to pop up from behind a tumbleweed or cactus, turned back to the conversation. "Boris, what the Sam Hell are you talking about? You don't know this kid's father."

Boris looked at his friend as he squeezed the boy's shoulder reassuringly. "Yessir, Gary Wayne, I believe I do. You do, too, unless I'm woefully mistaken."

Gary Wayne gazed intently at the kid's face as if seeing him for the first time. A brief look of recognition crossed his faced, and he blinked twice. "Boy," he asked in almost a whisper, "what's your name?"

"Percy."

"Percy what?"

"Murratt."

Boris gave Gary Wayne an I-told-you-so look. "Percival Murratt, Gary."

Gary Wayne shook his head slowly and sighed. "You Jim's boy?"

"Jim Murratt, yes sir."

"Big Jim Murratt's boy," Gary Wayne ran his left hand through his hair as Boris nodded with a hint of a smile on his face. "I'll just be Goddamned."

III.

"Boris, what are we gonna do?" Gary Wayne and Boris had moved off from Percy and were pretending to check the harnesses on the horses prior to moving on.

"I don't know, Gary," Boris replied as he adjusted the blanket and padding under Valiant's saddle, "what are you suggesting?"

"Well, we cannot just leave Jim Murratt's boy out here in the wilderness; that's for damn sure."

"Well, that may be true, but we also cannot turn around and take him to Bretton," Boris reasoned, sliding his fingers under Valiant's straps to make sure they weren't too tight. "As you have spent the better part of the day reminding me, we have lost enough time on this little wilderness sojourn already."

"I ain't suggesting we do," Gary Wayne jerked Gringo's up-tugs enough to pull the saddle almost completely off the blanket and up the horse's neck, "but maybe we can take him with us. After all, he's got just as much right to hunt Lank down as me. Lank wasn't any better friend to Jim than he was to Ardiss, you know."

"That may be so," Boris finished tightening the straps on Valiant's saddle and moved over to readjust Gringo's saddle as Gary Wayne seemed oblivious to his mount's obvious discomfort. "However, taking him with us is just as impractical as escorting him to Bretton. Have you seen the boy's mule? Even if he could make the trip where the hell ever we're going, he won't be able to keep up. Bottom line is the boy will just slow us down."

Gary Wayne seemed to consider this, furrowing his brow and absently chewing his lower lip. Finally, he seemed to arrive at a decision. "Well, if we can't take him with us and we can't escort him to Bretton, we can take him back home. We're gonna have to talk to Laney anyway since she's the last person to see Lank."

"I reckon we can ask him," Boris glanced at the boy who was himself folding his blanket over his mule's back and preparing to ride, "but he don't seem like he'll be too keen to go back home after traveling all this time."

"Well, I reckon we'll just see about that," Gary Wayne averred. "Seems to me the boy don't have a lot of choice in the matter if we give him our say-so,"

Boris said nothing to this, simply smiled to himself and returned to Valiant's saddlebags.

"You boy!" Gary Wayne called over his shoulder, "Come here; we got to palaver."

IV.

Boris kept his distance while his fiery-tempered friend tried to reason with the boy. He pretended to take inventory of his saddlebags and studiously avoided meeting either of their eyes.

Gary Wayne seemed as nervous and awkward as a cherry. His feet shuffled erratically, and his hands fidgeted in the air while he tried his level best to stay calm and speak firmly. For his part, the boy remained aloof, staring blankly and slowly nodding his head as the older man explained in painstakingly awkward stammers that they were going to take the boy back to his mother.

"So you see," Gary Wayne was explaining, "I mean what I mean to say is that … Well, the fact is …um… Look, boy, we cannot take you to Bretton."

The boy nodded and smiled absently.

"I mean we'd like to, no doubt about that, but we're kind of in the middle of something here that we do not … I mean … We are under an obligation to find Lancaster… Mr. O'Loch … you know that … um, gentleman we were asking you about?"

Another slow nod.

"And if we turn around now, we run a very good chance of losing his trail."

The boy said nothing, just stared blankly at Gary Wayne.

"Now I know what you are thinking. We could take you with us."

The boy neither confirmed nor denied that he was thinking this.

"This cannot be," Gary Wayne explained. "Y-You have a mule, you see." His hands were either conducting a phantom orchestra or trying in vain to motion in the mule's direction.

"Lippy," the boy confirmed. "Ma gave him to me."

"Lippy, yes. Well, I'm afraid Lippy will not be able to keep up with our horses so we will not be able to catch up to Lank… Mr. O'Loch… um, if we have to keep slowing down for you."

"Lippy is much slower than a horse," the boy agreed. "He's a mule."

Boris tried, mostly successfully, to disguise his snicker as a sneeze. He could tell that Gary Wayne's fuse was just about spent.

"Yes," Gary Wayne pronounced every letter clearly and slowly, "Lippy is a mule. He cannot keep up with our horses so you cannot go with us to find Mr. O'Loch."

The boy smiled and nodded, and otherwise said nothing.

"So I am afraid we have no choice but to take you with us as far as your mother's place."

"No sir."

"That way you will not be lost out here in the Waste Land, and we can get more information from your mother about … what did you say?"

Boris tied down his saddlebags and prepared himself to divert Gary Wayne's inevitable diatribe.

The boy had that same steely look he had earlier when Gary Wayne had accused him of lying. "I said 'No sir' sir."

The boy may be feeble-minded, Boris thought, *but he has grit. I'll give him that. He will not be trifled with.*

Gary Wayne had reached the end of his patience again; Boris could all but see the steam works in his head over boiling and sending plumes from his ears. "You listen to me, boy," Gary Wayne's voice began to steadily rise in both pitch and volume, and his finger began poking furiously into the boy's chest with each successive word. "I will be damned if some pube is going to tell me what I will or will not do."

The boy did not so much as flinch from Gary Wayne's onslaught. He merely blinked patiently each time the older man's finger made contact with his flannel shirt and stared.

"If I aim to go to your mother's place and ask her about my quarry, that's exactly what I will do."

"Mister," the boy interrupted, "I don't begrudge you a trip to see my ma. I just prefer to go on my way to Bretton. I figure it can't be too far from here."

"Couple days ride," Boris interjected, "maybe three, four at the most on that mule."

Gary Wayne stared slack-jawed at his partner as if Boris had just quietly sheathed a boot knife between his shoulders.

The boy nodded his thanks at Boris and continued. "If I go back to Ma's place, I don't reckon Lippy'd make another trip out here, and there I'd be, so no sir; I would prefer to keep going, but I thank you for offering to help me."

Gary Wayne's face had become as red as his shirt. "Now you listen here, you ungrateful puke…"

"Gary Wayne," Boris moved in between his partner and the boy. "The boy has a point. We have no authority over him, and if his heart is set on Bretton, I suppose that is where he will go. Like as not, he would simply wait for us to bed down for the night and continue on his way while we slept."

The boy considered this with a look that told Boris that while he had not at all considered it before, that was of a certain his plan now.

"Your whole aim in taking the boy back to his mother is to ensure that we do not leave Jim Murratt's boy in the wilderness to die of exposure or worse."

"Well, sure, Boris" Gary Wayne's temper, as was his won't, was subsiding now as quickly as it rose, "so I am not entirely certain of your point in taking the boy's side here."

"Gary Wayne, I have not taken anyone's side; I am merely taking the world as it is. We cannot dictate to this boy, and we cannot in good conscience leave him to his own woefully deficient devices. We must, therefore, do what we can to smooth his passage." Boris turned to the boy. "Do you know your letters, boy? Can you read a map?"

"Yessir, I can read some. Gramps taught me maps and Ma taught me the Bible."

"Good," Boris went back to his horse and removed a ledger from his saddlebag. He returned and opened it to a blank page and pulled a pitiful stub of a pencil from his pants pocket.

"Here is where we are," Boris drew a circle with an X in the middle of the paper, checked his pocket watch, and noted the direction of the sun. He then drew an arrow in the top corner of the page and wrote "N" at one end and "S" at the other. He then drew another line through the middle marking "E" and "W" at either end.

"You need to travel east and a little south of here, and you will run into our campfire from last night." Boris drew a small x below the circled X and a little to the side.

The boy looked confused, and Gary Wayne motioned for his attention. "Just go straight that way." He pointed in the direction from which the two men had come. "You cannot miss it."

The boy nodded and looked back at the paper. Boris had drawn three more X's in a relatively straight line and finally another circle. He was just writing "B" in this circle. "You keep in that direction, son, and you cannot help but run into Bretton. When you get there, you ask for the sheriff, tell him Gary Wayne and Boris sent you, and then tell him who you are."

"Don't be surprised," Gary Wayne put in, "if he gives you a broom and shows you the stables."

The boy nodded, took the map, and folded it into his hip pocket. "I thank you both for your help," he said and stuck out his hand. Boris grasped it firmly, but Gary Wayne turned away and moved toward the horses and fiddled with the saddlebags.

"Don't be mounting up quite yet," he said as he returned with a canteen and a wrapped package. "You won't get very far without water and at least some food." He handed the boy the canteen and package. The boy unwrapped the bundle enough to see that it was half a loaf of not-too-stale bread. "Make it last," Gary Wayne said and then stuck his own hand out. His eyes widened a bit at the boy's grip.

Boris smiled at this and mounted Valiant.

"You're going to be awful thirsty this afternoon," Boris teased as Gary Wayne mounted Gringo, and they watched the boy riding his mule out of the campsite.

"I don't see why " Gary Wayne answered, "I gave him your canteen."

Chapter Five
Guernica

I.

She has been in this dank and musty cave for days ever since he left her here with a week's supply of rations.

"I will return as soon as possible," he said with his thick brogue. "I need to scout the terrain and make sure we are not under pursuit. There is a spring at the back of this cave, and the water is safe. I will be back before the food runs out."

That was four days ago. Sometimes, she thinks about going home, but she knows it has gone too far for that. Ardiss would never believe or forgive her now. Too much *sangre* under the bridge.

She sighs and looks again out of the cave towards the eastern horizon, brushing a strand of black hair from her eyes. The sun has almost risen to noon, and still no sign of him. No one would believe her. *Cada uno cuenta de la feria segun le va ella, she thinks. Everyone tells their own story. Why should they believe mine?*

Her family had owned and worked a modest plot of land outside Delicias, Chihuahua, raising *tomates* for generations, ever since her ancestors came with de Vaca to settle the territory and fell in love with the land. As a young girl, Guernica had hoped to marry one day and take over *la granja* when her father, Leonardo Gracia, grew too old to work the land himself. Sadly, however, that was not to be, for that was before the bad times, before Porfiriato.

Guernica sighs and turns away from the cave's opening. She moves deeper in to escape the sweltering heat of the desert sun, to the spring at the back where she dips a dented tin cup and moves again to her bedroll to lie down.

She still remembers the day of her fifteenth birthday when shortly after she had successfully beaten the donkey piñata into submission, the well-dressed men came to her father's house, waving a piece of paper they claimed came directly from Don Porfirio, himself, and granted their employer sole ownership of her father's land. The Gracias were, however, welcome to stay on and work the fields for Señor Malevolo as sharecroppers.

"What is it, Papi?" she asked, while her young friends, oblivious to the inane discussions of the adults, scrambled about gathering as many treats from the shattered donkey as their shirts and skirt-laps could hold.

Leonardo seemed not to hear his daughter. He stared blankly at the paper as the men walked into their *cuadra* to take inventory of the farm's livestock.

"Papi," little Guernica asked again, "What has happened?"

"El fin, hija" he said quietly, "Es el fin del mundo."

It may not have been the literal end of the world for Señor Gracia and his daughter, but it certainly marked the end of Guernica's childhood. Even more effectively than the shattered piñata spilling its sweets and toys on the ground outside their *casita,* while strange men in fancy clothes counted their livestock and appraised their ancestral land which was no longer theirs to own but still theirs to work.

Señor Malevolo did allow them to stay on as caretakers. He even permitted them to remain in the main house unless, of course, he and his *esposa*, a particularly sour looking woman in her late forties, were in residence. During such visits (which grew increasingly more frequent as Guernica grew into her young womanhood), Guernica and her father had set up pallets in the *cuadra* with the burro and the cow.

Not so different from this, Guernica thinks as she rolls to her side on her bedroll to better spy the cave's entrance. *A little drier, tal vez. But otherwise much the same.* The memories have done little to relieve her brown study; she sighs heavily and stares aimlessly out of the cave mouth into the past.

Desiderio Malevolo was in his sixties when Presidente Porfirio Diaz ceded him the Gracia farm to secure his financial support for the completion of the Central Mexican Railroad. Guernica remembers clearly the day he first strode onto what she continued to think of as their land. As his driver helped him out of his carriage, he motioned impatiently with his free hand for his stick, a polished black cane with a bone handle, which his wife, Dolores, handed to him with an irritated grumble. Though he was stooped, Guernica could see that he had once been imposingly tall, almost six feet, with broad shoulders now withered a bit from too many winters spent at leisure, and too few summers spent at hard work. His once firm belly now tended to paunch when not held in by a waistcoat half a size too small. He wore a dark gray suit with a black ribbon tied about his stiff white collar. His hair he wore long in the front, but heavily oiled and combed back, ineffectively hiding the thinning patch on his crown.

When Delores stepped from the carriage, she took her husband's arm and together they moved toward Leonardo and his daughter. Señora Malevolo was a large woman, twenty years her husband's junior, but Guernica could not tell by looking at her. Her dress seemed to fit almost as tightly around her oversized waist as her husband's waistcoat fit him. When the woman moved, the flesh beneath her dress seemed to ripple like water lapping ashore with every step. Guernica had to hide a chuckle behind a minor coughing fit when she saw the woman walk towards them.

Like two rutting cerdos, Guernica thought as she embarked on another coughing fit. Her father gently nudged her with his elbow and gave her a stern look.

When the new masters of the farm approached the Gracias, the old man merely nodded at Leonardo.

"The house is in order, I trust?" he asked as he surveyed the yard.

"Si, señor," Leonardo replied keeping his eyes cast low.

81

"Muy bien," Señor Malevolo nodded but still did not look at Leonardo turning his attention instead on Guernica. "When we are done here, you may return to the fields and finish your work there."

"Si, señor,"

The old man met Guernica's eyes, and she abruptly looked to the ground with a blush. He tried to smile, but the best he could manage was a crooked leer. Beside him, Delores noted this exchange with a sneer.

"You are the daughter," he asked.

"Si, Señor Malevolo," Guernica spoke softly.

"Please, *chica*," Señor Malevolo licked his lips with a slight slurp, "call me Desi."

Delores rolled her eyes and glared at Guernica but said nothing.

"And look at me when I speak to you." Again he tried to smile unsuccessfully. "I promise I won't bite."

Guernica turned her face towards the old man. He reached out his gnarled hand and stroked her cheek. Guernica closed her eyes to hide her revulsion.

"Such nice skin," he said, "Nice color, so soft."

"Gracias, Señor … Desi" Guernica opened her eyes, and Señor Malevolo grasped her chin firmly between his thumb and forefinger.

"See, *chica*, that was not so hard, was it?"

"No, Señor Desi," Guernica struggled to speak above a whisper.

"Open your mouth, *por favor*," To illustrate his desire, Señor Malevolo worked his finger into her mouth, still firmly grasping her chin with his thumb, and hooked it on her lower lip. Guernica slowly opened her mouth and once again turned her eyes away from the old man. "Look at me, *chica*," he said more firmly, pulling her mouth more fully open with his finger, "Do not make me tell you again."

Guernica's eyes began to water as she looked into the old man's leering face.

"Your daughter has good teeth, Señor Gracia." Señor Malevolo released Guernica's face and kept his eyes focused just below her chin. "Very beautiful, she is, too. You are to be congratulated."

"Gracias, Señor," Leonardo kept his voice low, but tone was clipped, as though speaking through gritted teeth.

"She will keep the house in order for us." Señor Malevolo seemed not to notice Leonardo's ire. "Delores could use the help in the kitchen and with the laundry. Isn't that so, *mi quierdo?*"

"If you say so, Desi," Delores' tone, however, said quite the opposite, and she glared even more sternly at the young woman before her husband.

"I do, *mi quierdo.* I believe this arrangement will work quite nicely for us all."

With that, Desiderio and Delores moved into the main house, leaving Leonardo and his daughter alone in the yard.

"Be wary of those two, *hija,*" Leonardo moved to put his arm comfortingly about his daughter's shoulders. "Do not let yourself be caught between them."

"Si, Papi," Guernica wiped her eyes.

"We must keep low to the ground, *hija.* Perhaps this storm will pass us by." Leonardo gently guided his daughter into the *cuadra* and closed the door behind them. "I am not hopeful, though."

II.

When he finally arrives, the moon has almost completed its journey across the sky. He wakes her up trying so hard to be silent. She believes his boot fell out of his hand as he tried to slowly remove it from his foot. He starts to swear but stops himself with a hiss. She can see him just in the cave's entrance, his white suit glowing in the moonlight like a *fantasma*.

"Is okay, Lankestar," she says softly, "I am not asleep."

"Aye, but ye were sure enough, I ken" he grumbles as he moves to her pallet. He bends down and gently brushes her hair out of her eyes. "Yes indeed," he says softly with a hint of a smile, "I see the Sandman has nae been long gone from your eyes."

"Non," Guernica says with a yawn, "I have been just lying here thinking."

"No good's ever come o'that," Lancaster replies through his own yawn. "What were ye thinking on? Ardiss?"

"At first, *si*, but mostly of Papa." Guernica raises from the pallet to a sitting position and pats the ground beside her, inviting Lancaster to sit.

He complies and begins working on his other boot. "Would ye be wanting to talk about it?"

"Non, Lankestar," Guernica smiles when she notices how silently he can do this when he isn't trying. "Just come to bed; you've been riding all day."

Lancaster grunts neither confirming nor denying this, but he stands long enough to remove his trousers and shirt, fold them carefully over his saddlebags, then lies down beside her in his bleached white union suit, throwing his arm around her from behind and cupping a breast. Guernica wriggles back into his embrace and yawns contently. "Did you discover what you sought?"

"I reckon so," he takes a deep breath, savoring the fragrance of her hair: light soap and fain't sweat. "Laney had nae seen any men, so either Ardiss has nae sent out pursuit, which I deem is

84

unlikely, or he sent them out later than would seem best. I suspect the latter would be more in keeping with the Ardiss I know. He will not disgrace his honor. Though it pains him, he will send pursuit. His moral delay, though, has given us time to escape."

"*Sí*," Guernica says quietly. "Is that his aim, do you think? To give us time?"

"I wot it is at that," Lancaster's voice, too, grows quiet, contemplative.

The two lie together in the dark cave, each engrossed in their own thoughts. Lancaster can feel Guernica trying to hold in the sound of her sobbing. He gives no indication he knows.

She will speak when she needs to, he thinks.

"He took advantage of me," Guernica voice trembles.

"Ardiss?" *Nae, God, not him, please. I do not wish to kill him.*

"Non, not Ardeess," she pauses, gathering will, "Señor Malevolo."

"Who?"

III.

It happened two years after the Malevolos took over the farm. Guernica had blossomed into a fine young woman. She was known throughout Delicias as the most charming girl in all of Chihuaha, slim of figure, light of foot, with an easy smile that brightened any room. The village gossips devoted much of their laundry days to speculating over which of their young men Guernica would accept as her *novio*, but so far she had shown little interest in any man other than her father to whom she was devoted.

The only time Guernica showed anything less than pure joy and grace was whenever the Malevolos were in residence. Then her smile faded, her step grew heavy, and her shoulders slumped.

One day, after they had been in residence two weeks, Guernica was wiping down the table after Desiderio and his wife had broken their fast. She first used a rag to wipe the crumbs from the table to the floor. She could hear Desidero in the next room speaking to his wife, but she could not make out what he said.

As Guernica dipped her rag into a wooden pail filled with soapy water perched precariously on a three-legged stool, she heard Delores reply. "*No*, I will not allow it. *No*."

"I did not ask permission," Desidero said. "Do it or I will, I care not which."

There was a second or two of silence before Guernica heard Delores respond, in a much more subdued tone. "*Como desee*. It will be so."

Ringing her rag out thoroughly, Guernica began to carefully scrub the table with slow circular motions in the ensuing silence.

"You are doing it wrong, you stupid *chica*!" the harsh voice of Señora Malevolo startled her as she was dipping her rag into the pail for the third time, and she flinched, upsetting the bucket and splashing water on the floor.

"*Ay carajo*!" Delores yelled, "Now look at what you have done! I tell you every day, *pendeja*, sweep the floor before you wash, but you always know differently."

"I am sorry, *Señora*," Guernica took her rag and knelt to floor to sop up the spilled water. "I will clean it up."

Delores, though, would not be placated. "Now look at you!" Her voice quavered with inexplicable rage. "You are mixing the crumbs into the water and making a larger mess. Stop it now!" The larger woman stepped to where Guernica knelt under the table and fetched her kick to the backside with such force that Guernica fell over face first into the muck.

"Perhaps you need to see your mess closer up, you useless *chocha*." Delores nudged Guernica with her foot.

"*Si, señora*," Guernica spoke into the floorboards, tasting damp and soapy crumbs and feeling tears of shame and rage form at the corners of her eyes. "*Lo siento. Lo siento mucho*. Please do not kick me anymore. I will do better."

"See that you do," Delores used her foot to push Guernica further under the table, causing the waist of the girl's skirt to slide almost to her haunches, revealing the girl's undergarments. With a derisive snort, Delores turned from the table and left the dining area. She paused at the doorway and spoke over her shoulders. "You will be sleeping in the house from now on. Señor Malevolo wishes to have you nearby in case he needs you."

Guernica slowly pushed herself up from the floor, rearranging her skirt. "I do not wish to leave my *papi*," she responded trying her best to sound contrite.

"I do not recall asking your opinion of the matter, *puta*. You will sleep in the house from now on, starting tonight. Sleep in your old room. Do not lock the door." The older woman left the room. "Clean up that mess." She said over shoulder.

When Guernica told her father about the encounter, he pulled her to him in a hug and kissed the top of her head.

"You must be more careful, *hija*," he said quietly stroking the back of her head. "These are not people to anger. Do as you're told and draw no attention to yourself."

It is far too late for that, Guernica thought, though she remained silent.

"I do not think it is a good idea for you to sleep there. I do not like the way that man looks at you or the way that woman treats you, but I see no way around it." Leonardo sighed deeply and pushed his daughter back to look in her face. "You must promise me that you will lock your door every night."

"*Si, Papi,*" Guernica nodded, seeing no benefit in telling he father she had been expressly forbidden to lock her door.

So Guernica quietly moved back into her old room under the scornful eye of her mistress and the significantly less scornful eye of her mistress' husband. She spent the rest of the day occupied with her regular duties and tried to convince herself that there was nothing at all to worry about.

After she had cleared the evening meal from the table and cleaned the kitchen to Delores' begrudging satisfaction, though, the nervousness that had quietly lurked in the pit her belly all day began slowly to assert itself. Sitting in the corner of the kitchen reserved for her own meals, Guernica found she could stomach only a few bites before losing all interest in food. Through the window, she could spy her father's light in the *cuadra*. She desperately wished she could go there and lay down on her familiar pallet and go to sleep to the sound of her father's soft snores from the opposite corner.

Her reverie was broken by the sound of Delores' impatient sigh at the kitchen door. "It is getting late. Quit day dreaming and clean your dishes. It is time to close the house, and you need to be in the bed."

"*Si, señora,*" Guernica rose and took her plate to the scrap bucket.

"Look at all the food you are wasting, you stupid *bruja*!" She slapped at Guernica's head, but the younger woman ducked. "Do not put the food on your plate, if you do not mean to eat it."

"*Si, señora.*"

"Delores' snorted derisively. "Good. Clean up your mess and get ready for bed. Señor Malevolo will be in to make sure you are ready for bed shortly. Do not disappoint him."

"*Si, señora.*"

When Guernica finished the kitchen and made her way to her bedroom, she found Desiderio waiting for her. He stood by her bed wearing nothing but his night shirt and a leering grin. Despite her unease, Guernica found it difficult not to grin at the image of the old man's knobby knees quivering beneath his shirt and his pigeon-toed feet peeking out from beneath the hem.

"Oh there, you are, my dear." He said as Guernica stopped just inside the doorway. "Come in, come in. I was just checking to make sure you were settling in." When he raised his arm to beckon her in, Desiderio's night shirt shifted revealing more than just his knocking knees poking into the material of the shirt. Guernica, trying not to look too obviously lest he take it as an invitation, moved to the opposite side of the bed and made to light the candle on the bed table.

"I am fine, *señor*, she said, bending over the candle. "Thank you for your concern."

"Not at all, *mi querida*," Desiderio shuffled to the end of the bed and held the footboard for support. "I simply could not bear the thought of someone with your young and delicate frame sleeping on the floor of that drafty old shed."

As he moved around to Guernica's side of the bad, his joints cracked. When Guernica rose and turned around, the old man stood directly behind her, still leering. Guernica could see a tiny drop of saliva forming in the slightly drooped corner of his mouth. Guernica smiled and tried to duck around the old man, but he grabbed her about the waist with surprising strength.

"Did your *padre* not teach you it was polite to thank your betters for their favors?"

"*Si, señor, gracias.*" Guernica tried to gently remove Desiderio's fingers from the waist of her skirt, but they were like tempered iron. "*Muchas gracias.*" Her voice trembled, and she averted her eyes.

"*Denada, mi querido.*" Desiderio pulled Guernica so tightly to him she could feel every inch of his body beneath the shirt as if it weren't there at all. "*Denada* but words are easy. You need to show me your gratitude."

"*Por favor, señor.*" Guernica tried to keep her voice steady as Desiderio slowly backed her towards the bed. "Please, no. I will scream."

Desiderio pulled the waist of Guernica's skirt with enough force to rip it at the seam and tumble the girl to bed. Before she could scramble away from him, the old man grabbed her calf and pulled her under him as he straddled over her on the mattress.

"No, you won't scream, I think." He leaned and planted a kiss directly on Guernica's mouth before whispering into her ear. "For if you do, *puta*, I will have your father arrested and hung as a traitor." He snaked his hand beneath Guernica's blouse and groped clumsily at her breast. "Do not think I will not. I have the ear of Don Porfirio. El Presidente will listen."

"No," Guernica breathed. "Stop."

Desiderio removed his hand from her blouse, rose up, and slapped the girl across the face. "You do not tell me what to do, *puta*. I tell you." He rose off her and strode to the door with no sign of the quavering steps he had shown earlier. Drawing the latch across the door, he turned back to the bed with the whimpering girl sprawled across it. "And now I am telling you to take off the rest of your clothes and be quiet, or I will give you more to whimper about."

IV.

As Lancaster holds her from behind and Guernica tells her story, her voice gradually slowly breaks into sobs.

"I should have fought harder," she cries. "I should not have given in so quickly."

Lancaster gently tightens his hold around her shoulders and allows Guernica to weep silently until she drifts back into sleep.

Chapter Six
Gary Wayne & Boris

I.

They rode the rest of the day with little incident. About mid-afternoon, Gary Wayne swore he saw some kind of "fearsome critter" on the horizon.

"It looked for all the world," he claimed, "like a giant rabbit with horns on it like a deer or something." Gary Wayne held his hands about three feet apart to illustrate the impressive size of the bunny, then put both hands, fingers spread, to either side of his head to simulate antlers.

Boris reined Valiant in bringing him to a halt and stared blankly at his friend. "You saw a jackalope?" Boris asked doubtfully. "Out here? In the desert?"

"Well, I ain't ready to name it or nothing," Gary Wayne replied, "but I saw what I saw."

"Be careful, Gary Wayne," Boris tried to stifle his smile, "you are starting to sound like Pilsner."

Gary Wayne let out an irritated sigh, straightened his back in the saddle, and kicked Gringo to a walk, leaving Boris behind him. "Eddie Pilsner," Gary said over his shoulder, "claims he seen some kind of snake, leopard, lion thing sneaking around his ranch last year. Now you and I both know that's plain crazy."

Boris trotted Valiant up to Gary Wayne, who refused to look at him. "Crazier than a jackalope?"

Gary Wayne twisted his mouth into a sneer and finally turned to face Boris. "Yeah," he said irritatedly, "Everybody knows we ain't got lions and leopards here. But rabbits and antelopes is a whole 'nother issue."

"So let me get this straight," Boris cupped his chin in one hand and stared off into the horizon as if trying to will Gary Wayne's jackalope back, "You think an antelope tupped a rabbit and made a jackalope?"

"I don't make no claim about who tupped who. I'm just saying it ain't crazy talk like Eddie Pilsner."

"A rabbit," Boris spoke very slowly, "and an antelope?"

"Horses and jackasses make mules," Gary Wayne reasoned, "I don't see why a jackrabbit and an antelope cannot do it, too,"

Boris said nothing, just continued to ride alongside Gary Wayne.

"I ain't an idiot, Boris."

"Nobody said you was, Gary."

"It was a jackalope I seen," Gary Wayne nodded to himself, "and it ain't like it is the first strange thing I'd seen in my life."

And here we go, Boris thought. Again with Nat Greene.

But Gary Wayne just settled into silence, riding along, sunk in his own head.

II.

Bretton celebrated the new year with even more fanfare, if possible, than it did Thanksgiving and Christmas combined, or at least it seemed so to young Gary Wayne. Admittedly, though, it was his first time away from his family and home for any significant period, so it could well be that each successive holiday seemed much grander than the last.

Ardiss certainly seemed to take a particular pleasure in the New Year festivities. Popular tradition claimed that what one did during New Year's Day foreshadowed the year to come; therefore, Ardiss had made it a tradition that no one would eat their ham or collards or black-eyed peas until something interesting happened. "We don't want our year boring," he claimed at the beginning of every New Year's dinner, "so we got to make sure it won't be."

Ardiss' criteria for interesting, though, were very broad. While certainly a good street brawl had fit the bill once or twice and once a cattle stampede narrowly avoided had been clearly enough to bring on the victuals, most years' meals were presaged by dirty limericks, exaggerated tales of some deputy's exploits out in the wilds, or once even Eddie Pilsner's crude, hand-drawn interpretation of the snake/lion beast he claimed was draining his cows dry.

New Year's dinner was held each year in St. George's Episcopal Church. This year, Gary Wayne and Boris, only recently promoted to the kitchen staff, were both working the chow line which ran down the east side of the fellowship hall. As the townspeople filed through the line holding their tin plates out, Boris served the meat and cornbread while Gary Wayne spooned collard greens and black-eyed peas.

When the last person was served, Big Jim Murratt, standing protectively behind his very pregnant wife, Elaine; and had taken his place. Gary Wayne and Boris were allowed to make as good a plate as they could from the leftovers and eat it leaning against the back wall as best they could manage once the sheriff allowed the dinner to begin. There were just enough of the peas and greens to split into two almost decent portions, but they had to split the last piece of cornbread and the final slice of baked ham that Gary Wayne had managed to save back.

As the two boys carried their plates to the back and took their places against the wall, Ardiss rose, tapping his knife against his glass of tea until the hall reached some semblance of silence.

"I'd like to thank you all for coming and helping me and Gwen celebrate the new year this afternoon." He paused long enough to set his glass and knife back on the table and to allow the applause to die down a little. To his right, Guernica smiled shyly and nodded her head, blushing faintly at the attention. Lancaster, sitting beside her, gave her a reassuring pat on her shoulder as Ardiss continued. "Before we get started," here he turned to his left and spoke to the Rev. Tallison, "Merle, will you lead us on with a few words?"

Rev. Tallison smiled thinly, as he did every year, and rose slowly to stand beside his friend. He looked uncomfortably about the congregation, smoothing his black frock coat, and nervously flicked a strand of blond hair from his eyes as he towered at least a foot over the sheriff.

"Let us pray." The reverend's voice rose with the last word so that he seemed to be asking permission. As everyone lowered their heads, he continued:

"Lord Jesus Christ our God, You, who blessed the five loaves in the wilderness and fed the multitudes of men, women, and children, also bless these, Your gifts, and increase them for the hungry. Grant us also, as we stand at the beginning of this new year, the comfort of Your presence and guidance as we face the future. In the midst of life's temptations and the pull of our stubborn self-will, help us not to lose our way but to have the courage to do what is right in Your sight, regardless of the cost. This we ask in the name of our Lord and Saviour, who by His death and resurrection has given us hope both for this world and the world to come. Amen."

As the congregation murmured their own amens, Rev. Tallison sank slowly to his seat. "Not this year, apparently," he muttered as he slid his chair closer to the table, though Gary Wayne, at the back of the fellowship hall, admitted to himself that he could well have been answering an unheard question or muttered something else entirely.

"As I'm sure you know," Ardiss explained after the reverend was settled in, "it is our tradition to ensure that we don't all just die of boredom out here in the wilderness, to make sure we start our new year with exhilaration. To this end, we cannot partake of our New Year's feast until at least one person can provide us with some noteworthy div…"

Ardiss' speech was interrupted by the sudden crack of the double doors in the rear of the hall slamming into their frame, followed by a deep-throated chuckle.

"Well, I reckon you'll all be eating directly then," the newcomer laughed.

Gary Wayne, along with the rest of the startled congregation, turned to see a giant of a ruddy-faced man striding purposefully toward the front of the hall. He stood at least seven feet tall and was as broad across the shoulders as an ox. Beneath a leather vest, he wore an olive shirt open to his chest and tucked into a pair of trail-dusted jeans. He bore a pair of guns slung low on his hips.

"Who might you be, friend?" Ardiss' smile never wavered. Gary Wayne was sure he was the only person in the hall not startled by the stranger's entrance.

"Name's Greene," the newcomer replied not breaking his stride until he was within an arm's reach of the sheriff. "Nathaniel Greene. My friends call me Nat." He paused. "You can call me Mr. Greene."

Ardiss' smile wavered for only a second. "Well, then, Mr. Greene. Come, share our meal, and tell us what brings you to our little corner of the Waste."

Mr. Greene turned his gaze over the hall with a mocking sneer. "No thank you, Mr. Drake. I will not eat your meat, nor will I taste your drink. I will simply do what I come here to do and be on my way so your fine folks can enjoy what's left of their dinner in peace."

Ardiss' smile widened, but even from the back of the room, Gary Wayne could see the steely gaze behind his cold blue eyes.

Gary Wayne would later swear the temperature in the hall dropped a few degrees before Ardiss replied to this latest insult.

The Reverend Tallison muttered something under his breath that Gary Wayne could not make out, and Ardiss nodded before taking a deep breath. "And what is it, friend, you wish to do here?"

"I intend to set things right," the stranger said, and what happened next seemed to Gary Wayne to happen in a blur. Without taking his eyes from Ardiss, Nat Greene drew his gun from his hip with his right hand and leveled it at his host's chest, cocking the hammer with his thumb; his left hand, meanwhile, flicked out across his chest beneath his gun to Ardiss' right. At almost the same time, Lancaster let out a gasp as a heavy black orb hit him square in the chest, his chair fell backward, and his gun skittered across the table. Guernica screamed, and many of the patrons followed suit.

"No sir, Mr. O'Loch," Greene said keeping his eyes locked with Ardiss', "I do not believe your services will be needed today. I believe I can take care of my business with Mr. Drake just fine by myself, thank you kindly."

Lancaster merely grunted as he tried to regain his breath, Guernica helping him back to his chair as Caleb picked up the lead ball Greene had thrown and set it upon the table.

"What do you want, Mr. Greene?" Ardiss asked calmly as if offering his guest a beer, ignoring the cocked gun.

"I merely aim to deliver a message and a gift and be on my way."

"Well, then, sir, deliver them and be done with it."

Greene smiled coldly. "Mordecai sends his regards and asks that you have this back." Nat Greene's finger tightened on the trigger, and the hall erupted with the sound of gunfire as Ardiss dove to his right and sank to his knees, drawing his own gun. When he took aim, though, Greene lay face down, and Gary Wayne stood over him, smoke curling out of the barrel of his own pistol. When it was clear that Greene was down and that Ardiss was safe, Gary Wayne slowly released the hammer of the gun and handed it back to Deputy Eric Garan. "Sorry, sir," Gary Wayne explained, "I probably ought to have asked before taking your gun like that," Eric's free hand went to his unexpectedly empty holster, and he looked confusedly back at Gary Wayne, "but I had to take my chance when it come."

"Th-that's all right, son," Eric said looking down to make doubly sure that this was his gun and that his holster was indeed as empty as his hand said it was. "That's perfectly all right."

The rest of the gathered townspeople, who now understood what had happened, slowly clapped their hands as Ardiss stepped from around the table, walked to his nephew, and pulled him into an embrace, slapping him heartily on his back as he did it.

"Well, Mr. Orkney," Ardiss said with a laugh, "it would appear that I owe you my life this afternoon, thanks to your quick thinking and sharp shooting."

"Well, sir," Gary Wayne blushed, "I didn't do nothing nobody else wouldn't a'done. I seen him up there, not paying any attention to me, so I grabbed Mr. Garan's gun and got the drop on him is all."

Before Ardiss could respond, Eric, who had knelt down on his haunches to examine the body, spoke up. "Why ain't there no blood?"

Ardiss turned to his deputy with a question in his eyes.

"Look for yourself, Ardiss," Eric motioned to the form at his feet, "there ain't nothing there. If it weren't for his vest and shirt being blowed out, I'd say Gary Wayne missed and scared him to death."

At this, a low deep chuckle rose from the crumpled body at their feet. Eric fell back on his ass and slid into his wife, Enid's legs. Gary Wayne and Ardiss, however, stood their ground, though Gary Wayne's face paled just a little when the body at their feet rose to all fours. Once again, the hall fell silent except for Nat Greene's booming laughter. The giant man rose to his feet, dusted himself off, and turned to glare at the boy who had shot him. Throughout the hall, came the sounds of hands pulling leather.

"Sharp shooting?" Nat Greene let out another bellow. "Really, Ardiss? How hard could it be to shoot a man in the back?" He turned to glare down at Gary Wayne. "Who is this little cock-sucker thinks back-shots make heroes?"

Gary Wayne bristled at this, bucked up his chest, and stepped up to the stranger. "My name," he said, "is Gary Wayne Orkney, and …"

"And he is a duly appointed officer of the law in Bretton," Ardiss finished. "Furthermore, I'm afraid we don't stand on ceremony here. If someone attempts to assassinate an elected official, we don't much mind whether they're front-shot, back-shot, or side-shot, so long as they're shot."

"Well, sir," Greene responded, continuing to stare down at an unflinching Gary Wayne, "where I'm from, only a coward or a woman can get away with shooting a man in the back. Which are you?"

Gary Wayne's face filled with blood and his jaw set firmly, but before he could try to draw someone else's gun, Ardiss gently pushed the young man back and stepped between them.

"Mr. Greene, you appear to have received a belated Christmas miracle," Ardiss' voice seemed an odd mixture of patience, irritation, and amusement. "I suggest you count your blessings, confess yours sins, and get the hell out of my town, before my hot-headed young deputy here shows you once again how much of a cowardly woman he is not."

Greene seemed not to hear Ardiss. "I demand satisfaction from this squint."

It was Ardiss' turn to chuckle now. "I am afraid, sir, that you are in no position to demand a thing. Except for a cleared path to the door."

"I have no objection," Gary Wayne said, bending down to help Deputy Garan back to his feet. "If this man wants a fight, I will give it to him." At this, he turned to meet the giant's eyes. "What are your terms, sir?"

Nat Greene smiled. "My terms are these: You take a year to enjoy your newfound manhood. We will meet again, one year from today, in my territory and see if the fates smile on you as they have on me today."

"I do not understand," Gary Wayne admitted.

"It is very simple, son," Nat Greene's smile widened, "We have had but half a duel; you took your shot. In one year's time, I will take mine."

"That's absurd," Eric Garan called from behind Gary Wayne. "That ain't no proper gunfight."

"Nor was this," Greene countered.

Garan turned to his sheriff. "Ardiss, you can't permit this. It's foolishness."

"Indeed, it is," Ardiss agreed. "I will not allow it."

Gary Wayne turned to Ardiss. "With all due respect, sir, unless you tie me to the bed in a jail cell, I do not see what you can or cannot do about it if I accept his terms." Here he turned back to his challenger. "And I do accept his terms."

"In one year then," Greene said as the crowd parted and he made his way back to the hall's doors, "I shall send my second for you. Look for him after Christmas."

After the intruder left, the congregation turned back to their plates and ate their meals in relative silence. This year's meal had seen an assassination attempt, a resurrection, an impromptu deputizing, and a one-sided duel planned, suggesting (according to Ardiss' reasoning) a most notable year to come, few dared to speculate upon it or seemed comfortable discussing it so close to the young man seemingly doomed to enjoy but a year of his adulthood before surely falling under Nat Greene's fire.

III.

Sitting astride Valiant, Boris looked over his shoulder to where Gary Wayne and Gringo had fallen behind over the last hour. His friend seemed to be staring blankly out over the desert, and he was chewing the inside of his mouth as he had done whenever he was deep in thought for as long as Boris could remember. He felt briefly guilty for riding Gary Wayne about the jackalope earlier; Boris knew Gary Wayne had been obsessively vocal about finding Lancaster and exacting vengeance for his brother. Some of Gary Wayne's ideas about the proper disposition of Lancaster's remains once he was caught, tried, and justly hung had made Boris question his friend's mental soundness (one such suggestion, for instance, involved stretching Lancaster's skin into something called a cod-sock). Given this unhealthy fascination, Boris knew he should've been more sympathetic to Gary Wayne's distraction regardless of how silly it seemed at the time. He also knew that it would be fruitless to bring it up again. If he tried, Gary Wayne would simply answer with a grunt, and refuse to elaborate. Once shot down, most people, Gary Wayne included, very rarely got up again.

Most people that is, except Nat Greene. Boris knew that the jackalope had reminded Gary Wayne of the Nat Greene incident. This was another reason Boris should've feigned more interest in Gary Wayne's fearsome critter. Had he not questioned what Gary Wayne claimed to have seen, Gary Wayne would, himself, not felt the need to justify it. Now Boris' pard was falling behind, and it was obvious he was thinking about the day he was deputized.

Boris knew exactly what Gary Wayne was thinking. He remembered that day as well, the interrupted New Year's dinner (Boris had been just on the verge of amusing the townspeople with his story of finding a four-leaf clover growing out of a horse biscuit last week). He remembered the preternaturally silent dinner afterwards (Nat Greene's entrance and its sequel drastically lowered the currency of Boris' clover in shit story).

After everyone had finished their meals, and Reverend Tallison had once again blessed the congregation and sent them off to encounter whatever the new year had in store for them, Ardiss somberly approached Gary Wayne, who sat in the back of the hall beside Boris again, quietly scraping the last of his food into his mouth.

"Mr. Orkney," He leaned over and spoke in not quite a whisper, "if you would be so kind as to accompany me across the street, there is something I need to discuss with you."

"Sure thing, Mr. Drake," Gary Wayne replied as he swallowed the last of his dinner.

Ardiss nodded and proceeded on to the door. As he opened it and prepared to step into the street, he looked back over his shoulder. "Bring Boris, too," He said. "we'll have need of him."

After cleaning up the tables and putting the fellowship hall back into order, Gary Wayne and Boris crossed the dusty street to meet Ardiss. They walked past the jailhouse and entered The Caring Lion Saloon, where Ardiss and his men could be found more often than not, holding court around the faded poker table in back rather than next door pushing papers and riding nursemaid over town drunks locked safely away in a cell. Caleb Ecton, who in addition to being Ardiss' Chief Deputy was also the owner and proprietor of the saloon, had long ago cut a doorway connecting the back storeroom with Ardiss' office in the adjacent jailhouse.

"You boys can't be in here," the bartender, Shanghai Denny, glared at them and waved the rag he used to wipe the counter at them. "You're too young. Oughta have your hides tanned just for thinking about it."

"It's okay, Denny," Ardiss said from the back of the room, he and Merle were playing double solitaire in the shadowed alcove in back of the room. "I asked them to come."

Shanghai Denny didn't say anything to this, just grunted his disapproval and began wiping down the counter again, shaking his head. Ardiss waved the boys over to the table, as Merle collected the cards and reshuffled them. He handed the deck to Gary Wayne, who cut it with his right hand. Merle looked at the bottom card in Gary Wayne's hand, the six of clubs, and nodded to Ardiss before reshuffling the deck and dealing one card face down to each player save himself.

"The game," he announced in his almost quavering voice, "is Five Card Stud, nothing wild."

"I hate stud," Gary Wayne said irritably, forgetting momentarily who had invited him. He could hear Caleb's voice growling in the back of his mind. *Stupid dolt, you're sitting at table with the sheriff, cully, not some inbred slop-boy. If he wants to play Chicago Bitch naked and with his toes, you'll strip and say thanks.*

"Stud poker," Ardiss said, "is as close to life as any game ever gets. You don't get second chances, and you have to choose based on your best guess and judgment."

Merle dealt a card face up to each player. Ardiss' face showed only a hint of a frown when he received the four of clubs. Boris received the four of diamonds, and Merle looked twice when he laid six of clubs in front of Gary Wayne.

"Are you not going to play, Reverend?" Boris asked taking note of the empty patch of green felt in front of the dealer.

"Cards are the devil's playthings, son," Merle said with an almost imperceptible wink. "I believe you have the low card; it's your bet."

Boris looked at his hole card and kicked in two coppers, and the betting moved on to Ardiss, who merely glanced at his four of clubs and called. Gary Wayne raised the bet by another two pennies, and his companions each called. Merle dealt the third cards.

He laid the one-eyed jack of hearts in front of Ardiss, who then turned the corner of his hole card and peeked. He glanced fleetingly back at his jack and looked across the table at Gary Wayne. "You impressed me this morning Mr. Orkney. Not many boys your age would've had the grit to stand up to an armed man in a crowded hall."

"Or men," Merle added as he laid the ten of clubs in front of Boris and the jack of spades in front of Gary Wayne. "Your bet, Mr. Orkney."

Gary Wayne opened with a nickel. "Oh, I don't know, Mr. Drake. Boris here woulda done it if I hadn't. I just had a better chance at Eric's … I mean Deputy Garan's gun." Boris looked at Gary Wayne's bold opening and threw him a questioning look but met his bet. Ardiss smiled to himself, gently shook his head and did the same. Neither raised.

"You also," Ardiss continued as Merle dealt the next round, "managed to make a liar of me."

"I do not understand," Gary Wayne said as he looked at Ardiss' king of diamonds and Boris' king of spades. He smiled at the six of spades Merle had dealt him. The pair this made with his six of clubs meant he got to open betting again. He threw in another nickel. Boris called, and the bet moved to Ardiss.

"Well," Ardiss said, matching the bet and raising it another copper, "I couldn't very well let Greene think a civilian had fired on him from behind. Next time you left the confines of the town, he be likely to return the favor."

"What's to stop him now?" Boris asked, frowning at the four of spades Merle handed him. Ardiss' man with the axe paired with his new king of hearts, beat his pair of fours.

"Well, for starters," Gary Wayne said grinning at the six of hearts now giving him a three of a kind showing, "he give his word he wouldn't." He threw another nickel into the pot.

"Oh sure," Boris said, "because a man who'd endanger women and children by pulling a gun on the sheriff in the middle of a town gathering is clearly a man of honor. I fold, by the way." He flipped his hole card, revealing a seven of clubs and pushed his hand away from him toward the pot.

"I cannot say that anything will stop him, for true," Ardiss said meeting the nickel and throwing in an extra penny. "However, believing that your actions are backed by my Riders and me may make him cautious. If he attacks you outside of the foolish bargain you made with him, he will believe that my men and I will descend on him and exact our vengeance."

"Wouldn't you?" Gary Wayne asked as he met the raise and raised another penny.

"I would, surely," Ardiss said examining his cards. "You are my kinsman, and I am fairly fond of you." He winked at Merle, who simply rolled his eyes and peered at Ardiss' hand. Ardiss tossed in two more pennies. "I cannot speak for my men, though. Some would retaliate out of a respect for justice. Others might think it was deserved since you did back-shoot the man."

Gary Wayne frowned a little as he raised the bet again by a penny. "Well, he was going to kill you."

"Indeed, he was," Ardiss agreed, "and I am sure most of the Riders would avenge you. However, all of this is empty speculation. I do not like having deceived anyone, even a brigand, and harrier such as Greene. Therefore, I am, as of now, deputizing you. Congratulations, Mr. Orkney, you have earned your badge." Ardiss tossed in another cent. "I call, by the way. Let us see your cards, sir."

Still stunned, Gary Wayne turned his hold card revealing the jack of clubs. Ardiss turned his remaining card and showed the jack of hearts.

Merle looked at Ardiss' two jacks and bit his lip. "It would appear," he said, "that someone does not like you, Ardiss."

"I am quite certain that many people do not, Merle," Ardiss replied. "It comes with the job, I'm afraid." He smiled at Gary Wayne and pushed the pot across the table to the young man. "It would appear, sir, that this is your lucky day. Your full house beats my two pair, I believe."

"Th-thank you, sir," Gary Wayne stammered as he finished pulling the pot to himself and began transferring the coins to his belt purse.

"And now, Boris," Ardiss turned to the other young man, "if you will witness, and the good reverend here will officiate, I would like to get this young man sworn in."

Merle turned and reached behind him and pulled his Bible from the bar as Boris nodded his head. Ardiss called Shanghai Denny over to be a second witness then had Gary Wayne lay his hand on Merle's Bible and had him swear to uphold the law and justice to the best of his ability and to serve and protect the people over which he was given authority. After Gary Wayne did this, Boris and Shanghai Denny signed the witness sheet, and Ardiss reached into his vest pocket and removed a tin badge.

"It looks like you have just won about ten dollars tonight," he observed as he pinned the badge to Gary Wayne's shirt over his left breast. "I suggest you use it to purchase some appropriate gear."

"Yessir," Gary Wayne said.

"You will need to be apprenticed," Ardiss added. "You need someone to show you the ropes and ease you into the job." Ardiss looked at Merle. "Who do you think, Merle? Eric? Big Jim?"

Merle, who had returned to his place at the card table, was idly flipping cards into a pile. When Ardiss spoke to him, Merle flipped the jack of hearts onto the pile. "I don't think so," he replied.

IV.

Now, years later, Boris crested a hill overlooking a valley cut from a long dried up river and turned back to see Gary Wayne slowly catching up with him, still chewing the inside of his cheek and staring blankly into the past.

Yeah, it's hard to keep the anger burning when you think about that, isn't it Gary Wayne? No matter what the man did in the heat of passion, it cannot completely erase what he did for you as a younger man, can it?

Boris scanned the terrain below the hill and across the ravine. The sun was getting on to noon, and it was about time they gave their mounts a rest. With any luck, they might find that the riverbed below them was not entirely dry, and they could water themselves and the horses.

You may not be able to forgive him, but neither can you entirely condemn him. Maybe Merle knew what he was doing when he suggested you apprentice to Lancaster.

Something on the upslope across the river caught his eye, a dark spot in the wall of the ravine. Boris shaded his eyes with his hands for a better look. When this proved little better, he reached into his saddle bag and removed a pair of small, leather covered brass binoculars and raised them to his eyes. When he looked at the shadow again, he smiled.

"Gary Wayne!" he called over his shoulder, sure that the breeze would carry his voice away from the ravine and toward his partner. "Hurry up and get over here. You need to see this."

On the other side of the ravine, about halfway up the rise, Boris had found a cave, and he could see what might be relatively fresh tracks leading into it.

Chapter Seven
Percy

I.

I travelled the way them gunslingers told me to for most of the morning. Sure enough, round about the time I started getting hungry again, I run up on their old campfire. I stopped for a little, long enough to take a swig or two from the canteen Redhead give me and to rip a piece of the bread off for me and strap Lippy's feedbag onto him. Lippy didn't seem too impressed with the measly drops of water I give him, but I told him he'd have to just make do until we got to Bretton. We had to spread the canteen out as much as possible.

It felt a little strange to put the sun at my back after I stopped for lunch, but Redhead seemed pretty sure of himself, and that map Slouch Hat give me said go straight on, so I did. Well, long about sundown, me and Lippy, we come up on their next campsite, and since it was about to be getting too dark to see, I figured it'd be best just to make camp there for the night.

I unpacked my gear and fed Lippy from his bag again before turning my mind to a fire. There wasn't no wood left but some charred little stubs. At first, I was stymied; it was gonna be one cold night if I didn't have a fire, and I didn't relish having to snuggle up to Lippy again. He was warm, sure enough, but he smelled something awful.

Now wait a minute, I thunk to myself. *If they had a fire last night, they had to find wood somewhere. Unless Gramps helped them, too.* I didn't think that last was too likely; Gramps wasn't too fond of strangers, so I told Lippy I'd be back directly, took Gramps' hatchet, and walked off in search of wood.

Well, I hadn't gone five minutes out from camp before I heard what sounded like running water somewhere. Now I admit I don't know much, but I knowed I was in a desert, and they ain't famous for their water, so I decided to investigate. If there was water, I figured there was also a chance of fish for dinner instead of bread.

Sure enough, there was a little stream not even a quarter mile from camp, and what was more, there was a few little scrub trees growing right up next to it. It wasn't easy, but I managed to find me a branch on one that wasn't too twisted and run fairly straight, so I took the hatchet to it, rolled up my pants legs (ain't nothing worse than having to sleep in wet pants legs), took off my boots, and kinda sidled into the water to wait for a fish.

It wasn't too long at all before I seen a little one swimming my way. I got all set to gig it, but I just wasn't fast enough. I missed it by just a hair, then my stick slipped on one of the creek rocks, and I fell backside first right into stream. I was sure glad Ma wasn't around to hear what I said next. I ain't never had a taste for castor oil.

"You know," a laughing voice said from the other bank, "there are better ways to catch a dinner."

I looked up and seen an old man sitting cross-legged under another scrub tree. At first, I thought he was Gramps again, but when I looked closer, I seen he wasn't nothing like Gramps. He was all dressed in leather, and his hair was mostly white, but it still had some black in it, and it was tied in two pigtails that hung down to both shoulders.

"This is how my Gramps taught me." I wanted to ask him what he meant, but Ma told me not to ask no questions, so I just shrugged. "You're an Indian," I added.

"No, Pale Face," he slowly rose up and limped into the water, "I am a Human Being, one of The People."

I didn't know what he meant so I just grunted. He waded out to the middle of the stream and stood next to me.

"Give me your stick." Before I could hand it to him, he grabbed it from me and looked down at his feet. There was a whole school of fish swimming all around us now. I hadn't even seen them coming.

The old man muttered something under his breath and jabbed my spear into the water four times. When he brung it up again, there was three fish on it stacked on top of each other. "It's in the wrist," he said as he walked back to the bank carrying my spear and the fish and favoring his left leg. I just stood where I was, wondering how Ma would feel if I beat up an old cripple and stole his fish. I had just about decided against it since there wasn't likely to be no churches anywhere nearby when the old man got to his tree and turned around.

"Are you coming?" he waved the spear in my direction. "These fish cannot eat themselves, and I do not have all night."

II.

I had left my shoes on the other side of the creek, and even at sunset, the desert sand was awful hot on my toes. Fortunately, he didn't lead me too far away. He had a tepee set up just over the hill from the creek, about five minutes off. For a fella with a limp, he sure could move fast. By the time I got to his tent, he had already disappeared inside it.

I stood outside wondering what to do next, and, to tell God's honest truth, cursing Ma for making me make that stupid promise or else I could just ask him if I could come in when he stuck his head out of the tent flap.

"Is it against your religion to enter a tepee, Pale Face?" he asked me.

"No, sir," I said.

"Do you have some ritual you must perform before you enter a dwelling?"

"No, sir," I said.

"Alright, then," he nodded and ducked his head back in the tent, but I wasn't sure if that was an invitation or not, so I still didn't know whether I should just go in, too, or wait.

"What is your name, Pale Face?" the old man asked from inside.

"Percy," I said. "Percy Murratt."

"Do I need to invite you in, Percypercymurratt?"

"Yes, sir," I said. "I think so."

"Well, Percypercymurratt, please come in and have a meal with me," he said.

It didn't take him long to clean and cook the fish. He had kept his fire embers smoldering while he'd been out. We sat across from each other in his tepee with the fire pit in between us. As we ate, I couldn't help but notice how he'd every now and then wince and grab his upper left thigh when he didn't think I was looking. I think he caught me staring once, but he didn't say nothing about it, just fingered more fish into his mouth.

112

"Do you know how the world was made?" he asked around his food as he chewed.

"Ma told me all about it when I was little," I replied. "I also read the bible a bit when I was learning my letters."

The old man just nodded silently, so I continued. "God done it in seven days," I said. "At first, there wasn't nothing, but God, he separated heaven and earth. He said, 'Let there be light,' and it come when he looked at the water."

"Hmm," the old man threw the bones of his fish into the fire and motioned me to do the same. "Where did these waters come from?" he said.

"I reckon they come when he separated earth and heaven," I said, tossing my own bones into the fire. The fire sparked up real bright when I done it, and kind of startled me like.

"Your tale does not make sense, White Man," he reached behind him and pulled around a little leather bag. "This is earth," he winced as he kicked the dirt floor of his tepee. "You cannot drink earth. Where did the water come from? Where did the earth come from? Or the heavens?"

"God made them, I told you."

"No, you said he separated them one from another." He reached into his little bag and pulled out a long wooden pipe with gray feathers hanging from one end. "Then you said he created them after he separated them. How can someone make something that is already there?" He reached back in his bag for a thick smelling tobacco then started to fill his pipe.

"Ma said God can do anything."

"White Man's God is very powerful indeed if he can create something after it has been created." He lit his pipe using an ember from the fire and took a long draw from it. He passed the pipe to me. "You smoke with me, White Man," he said, "and I will tell you a tale."

I took the pipe from him and inhaled. I hadn't ever smoked before, but I had seen Gramps do it my whole life. He'd almost always smoke an old corn cob in the evening after dinner while Ma cleaned up. I don't remember him coughing that much, though.

The old man looked at me all serious like.

"The water and earth were always there, but it began with the water."

III.

The long before time was a time of chaos. The earth was covered with dry deserts and volcanoes. Into this chaos, the Great Sky Father sent the water, the Great River Daughter, to heal the earth. She came first as a trickle but soon grew into a torrent that cooled the volcanoes and soaked the earth.

From the water soaked earth, there grew a great Yucca tree. The River Daughter looked upon Yucca and was well pleased. She came to him, and they lay together, the tree and the water, and she carried his seeds throughout the land. Some of the seeds, those that took after their father the Yucca, grew into other trees and plants. Other seeds took after the River Daughter, now the River Mother. They had arms and legs and trunks like Father Yucca, but they were fluid and could move about like the River Mother. Indeed, when one of them was cut, muddy water flowed from it like spring water from the earth. These were the animals.

One animal was the greatest of all, for it most resembled both parents. It stood straight and tall like Father Yucca. In fact, its seed had not been carried downstream by River Mother. She had instead loosened the earth around Father Yucca's roots so that they could spread. As they spread, River Mother smoothed their skins, making their passage through the desert clay easier until they could break the surface of the earth and reach, like their father, to the sky.

Even though this animal had roots that sunk far into the ground and sprung from the roots of Father Yucca, his spirit moved like his mother. Sometimes he could be calm like River Mother when she trickles through a stream on a warm summer day. At other times, he could be treacherous and violent, as when River Mother brings the melted ice down from the mountain when winter is over, and spring has begun.

Only this animal could reason with ability close to that of Father Yucca and Great Sky Father. He was called, therefore, Man. But reason has two edges. It can help man achieve his higher nature, yes, but it also can tempt man to break his roots and call it freedom. This is what happened to man in the longbefore time when chaos was ending, and order began.

IV.

We passed that pipe back and forth, and it seemed like days that we set there, the old man talking and me listening to every word. After a while, I started to see his story played out in the smoke drifting up from his fire. I could see the tree and the river, and I watched plants grow, and people start to poke out of the ground. I tried shaking my head, but it didn't do nothing but make them people sway back and forth, waving their hands in the air and looking like they was crying and angry about being stuck in the ground like that.

I figured I could relate on account of how many times I had found myself stuck in the river mud after trying too long to spear a fish. I remembered Gramps would always laugh at me as he pulled me free.

"I don't know why you're squalling so," he'd say, "There're worse things to be than stuck with your feet in the ground. Most folks," and here he'd glance out to Pa's grave, "ought to spend more time there."

When I looked back across the fire pit at the old man, he looked like Gramps again but only for a second when the smoke come in between us. I felt like it was Gramps telling me to pay more attention, so I done that.

"One day Coyote spoke to the Men. Coyote grew from the seeds that were carried by River Mother, so his feet were not bound to the earth and he could move freely. Coyote always traveled near River Mother to be close to her nourishing waters, and he spoke of all the places he had seen, all the places River Mother flowed."

The old man paused here, drew on the pipe, and stared almost sadly into the flames. When he spoke next, his voice had a kind of choked up sound to it like he had inhaled too much smoke. "But Coyote was not Man's friend. He was jealous of the connection Man had to Father Yucca, for he desired to be the favorite. Eagle tried to warn man to pay little heed to Coyote, but after hearing Coyote's words, the people grew tired of being in one place. They, too, wanted to move around and follow their mother to see where she flowed. So they ignored the warnings of Eagle."

In the smoke, I saw the people reach below their feet with sickle blades and cut themselves free. When this happened, an air pocket in one of the firelogs split and a keening whistle, bout like a scream broke through.

"Father Yucca," the old man continued, "was heart-broken. And he wept, for he knew that when man left his roots behind, he would yearn for them evermore."

V.

The People travelled the length and breadth of River Mother's course. Each time, they stopped, River Mother asked them to remain and heal their roots so they could join again with Father Yucca. Many of the people did, but soon, others would remember Coyote's words, and they would feel the pull of River Mother's current, which even she could not control, and they desired to see more of the world.

Finally, the people were spread apart, and they began to speak differently and to look differently. Some even built boats when River Mother became Mother Ocean, and sailed to faraway lands, never to be heard from again. The others, who remained on the Land, became separated, and while they each called themselves The People, the words sounded different for each tribe: Cheyenne, Lakota, Apache, Arapahoe.

Finally, Man understood what Eagle had tried to tell him. Most places looked like most other places. Eagle had flown over the Land in all directions, and he knew this to be true. Man began to yearn for Father Yucca again, but he had wandered so far and so long that he had no way of finding Father Yucca. Eagle was very little help; he could tell man that Father Yucca was to the north or to the south, but giving directions from air does not help a traveler on land. Coyote pretended to help, but he was wily and had no desire to reunite Man with his Father. He led Man further and further away. Soon Apache blamed Arapahoe for leading him astray, and Cheyenne blamed Lakota. The People began to distrust each other, and Coyote encouraged this, often telling one tribe that another had dishonored them when no such dishonor occurred.

The Great Sky Father looked down upon his grandchildren and took pity on them.

"My family is divided," he said sadly. "I must bring them together again."

And so saying he spoke with his son, Father Yucca, and they agreed that such an endeavor would require the greatest of sacrifices. Father Yucca, therefore, gave up one of his branches and Great Sky Father carved it into a great knife. Father Yucca then gave up another branch, and Great Sky Father bent it into a long bow. Another branch Great Sky Father shaped into a dish, and another became a deep cup. He gave each of these into River Mother's care and instructed her to give one each to each tribe of Man.

"Now," Great Sky Father smiled to himself. "Man must work together in order to eat well, for one tribe will have the bow to kill buffalo while another must use the knife to clean and prepare the meat. A third tribe will provide the dish on which to eat, and the last tribe will have the grail to fill with water from River Mother and to add to the feast. When this happens, the connection between Man and Yucca will be remade."

"Let it be so," said Father Yucca, who now only had one or two branches left, but he feared his sacrifice would be for nothing.

VI.

As the old man talked, I felt my head get heavy. I tried to pay attention, but I musta dozed off at some point because next thing I knowed I was standing a few feet aways from this big old desert tree, what Gramps used to call Joshua's tree. I always wondered who Joshua was and why this tree of hisn wasn't at his house, but I never did get chance to ask him. Only difference is this tree kept losing its limbs. They turned into all these different things, a bow and a cup and stuff, and floated down this river next to the tree. While all this was going on, I could still hear the old man talking like he was far away, from the sky maybe.

"Coyote watched this from the scrub on the edge of the clearing." The old man said, and I could see just a few feet off, a coyote peeking from behind some low brown bushes. He looked in my direction, and I don't know if'n he seen me or not, but he hunkered down a bit more out of sight. "Though he had separated man from Father Yucca, he was no closer to replacing Man in Father Yucca's heart. When he saw the sacrifice of Father Yucca's limbs, Coyote grew angry with envy.

"'No matter what I do,' he said, 'Father Yucca still yearns for his disobedient children. Look at how he tears himself apart with his grief! I will show him that the true nature of Man is destructive and cold.'"

From behind the bush, I heard a snort and the coyote run off down the desert following the river. Then I knowed I was dreaming because next thing I wasn't in the clearing with Joshua's tree; I was in an Indian camp and the coyote was there with his snout up to this one Indian's ear. The Indian had a bow in his hand and every time he nodded his head at what Coyote said, he'd grip the bow tighter and pull it in towards him more.

Next thing I was in another camp and the coyote was whispering in the ear of another Indian. This one had been skinning a deer with a big ol' wooden knife. Every time he nodded his head, he'd look out towards the horizon with a scowl and squeeze the handle of the knife tight like he figured someone'd show up directly to take it.

The same thing happened in another camp where an Indian woman hid a wooden plate under her blanket after the coyote whispered to her. And in a fourth camp, this one Indian woman buried her wooden cup and didn't even mark where she done it so she could find it again.

"Coyote travelled to each tribe," the old man spoke again, "and spoke with the guardians of the relics.

"'The other tribes will be jealous of your treasure,' he told each guardian, 'for they work best together. Soon the other tribes will come to take it away from you.'

"When no tribes came, each guardian thought to himself, 'If the treasures work better together, should we not also try to take the others before the tribes come for ours?'

"They spoke to their chiefs, who saw in the prospect of more treasure, the opportunity for more power. Soon Man no longer desired to reunite with Father Yucca, River Mother, and the Great Sky Father; he sought to supplant them."

Then I seen Indians fighting on the plains. Sometimes, one group would get another's relic, but most times it ended in a draw, and nobody got nothing but grief. I seen other tribes argue with themselves about how to get the other relics, and they'd split off into new tribes and fight over their one relic. After a while, I seen that all these Indian tribes was wandering all over everywhere looking for the relics. (I knowed that one lady shoulda marked where she buried the cup with a rock or something at least).

"When the Great Sky Father saw how Man had squandered his gifts, he grew even sadder. He knew that now Man had fallen so far away from Father Yucca that they might never be reunited. 'The time has come,' he said, 'when no one wants gods and goddesses to nurture them.'

"Father Yucca, sagged down, twisting his trunk in his grief. 'We are driven into the darkness,' he cried. 'Man has lost his way, and we cannot help him find it. He has severed his connection to me and to the earth, and only heartbreak shall follow.'

"River Mother sighed, and her waters slowed. 'Soon,' she declared, 'summers will be flowerless, cows shall not give milk, and trees will bear no fruit. Oceans will be without fish, and poison will choke the rivers. Smoke will cover the earth, and the land will be covered in rock stacked to the sky. Man will weaken and have no shame: Judges will make unjust laws, honor will count for little, and warriors will betray each other and resort to thievery. There will come a time when there will be no more virtue left in this world.'

Then I seen men in long boats with yellow hair and horns in their heads burning villages and killing red and brown haired men. I seen men in metal suits beating other men in metal suits and burning more villages. I seen white men killing red men and red men killing each other. I seen white men beating brown men. I seen yellow men dressed funny and slicing each other up with swords. I seen yellow men and white men flying in the air dropping fire on each other from the sky, and I seen yellow haired men with blue eyes cooking brown haired men in ovens.

Then I seen it all again.

Gramps telling me to get up.

I seen the old man wince and rub his left leg.

"Don't be asking foolish questions," Ma told me, "if'n you see anything you don't understand."

"You're gonna need to ask a question or two before it's all over," Gramps said told me. "Wake up before it is."

The old man looked at me like he wanted something from me.

"You gotta ask the question," Gramps said.

"It'll get you killed," Ma countered.

The old man rubbed his leg and squeezed his thigh with a wince.

"All life is transitory," he said. "Even your children are not immortal."

VII.

I waked up in the clearing with Lippy biting my pants leg and tugging me. He was all brushed clean, and someone had filled his oat sack with more of them giant oats. I stood up, and I seen another cooked fish next to a smoldering campfire I hadn't ever made. I ate the fish and swallowed from my canteen what was all full now of cool water. My shoes was clean and set up next to my blanket, so I put them on. I knowed we still had days of desert riding ahead of us, so I folded my blanket for a saddle again, climbed up on Lippy, and headed out in the direction I figured Bretton was on account of the arrow someone had drawed in the dirt by the campfire.

When we passed where the old man's tepee was last night, I couldn't see hide nor hair of him to thank him for dinner and getting me back to camp safe. The ground looked like it hadn't even been walked on like he hadn't even been there, but this didn't raise no hackles on me. I knowed Indians are good at cleaning up after themselves like that.

Still when we passed the place, I got this funny feeling like I had forgot something but couldn't for the devil figure out what it was.

Chapter Eight
Rev. Tallison

I.

Will You speak to me today?

The old man stood before an open grave in the noon-day sun, his silhouette against the sky like that of a Joshua tree: long and thin, his spindly branch-like arms raised up beseechingly to the heavens. His black coat-tails and his shoulder-length thin and stringy hair, once blond, now white as snow, flew all about him like leaves caught in the slight breeze blowing in from the mesas and canyons just outside of town. He was tall, this man, well over six feet, but a lifetime of bending under doorways and stooping down to hear his parishioners had caused him to stand with a slight slump.

Take Your time; I can wait.

Opening his eyes, the old man stared directly into the sun as if into the face of the Almighty. He extended the fingers of each hand and slowly pulled them back into fists, grasping at something just out of reach.

As he stood thus silently, a crow cawed above his head, circled the graveyard twice, and swooped down, landing at the bottom of the open grave. It cawed once more, looking up from the floor at the old man staring blankly into the sky. It tilted its head to the left, then the right, and seemed to shrug before pecking into the hard packed earth and, after some struggle, pulling a worm and swallowing it whole.

The crow took wing again, perching in the clapboard headstone and looking down at the hand painted inscription:

GARRETT ORKNEY
BORN TOO LATE
DIED TOO SOON

The crow then surveyed the grave from its perch, seeming to measure the length, width, and depth with an exacting eye before nodding its approval, cawing once more, and flying off into the western sky.

Throughout this, the old man stood still, hands outstretched, fists clenched, eyes staring blankly into the sun. Tears formed at the corners of his eyes and traced rivulets down his temples.

Why do you not speak to me anymore? How have I displeased you? Will you not give me something?

A tugging at his sleeve roused him out of his reverie. He blinked three times, lowered his arms, and began to smooth out his coat, vest, and pants. His sleeve tugged again.

"Merle?"

The old man looked up again, "Yes?" he said with just a hint of a quaver.

"Merle? Over here." The old man looked to his right where a younger man (though by no means young) stood with his hand on the old man's coat sleeve.

This new man seemed to be anywhere from his mid-forties to his late fifties; out here, age was a hard thing to tell. Beneath his brown derby, the man's hair was cut short, dark brown, but with a light salting of gray at the temples. He wore what here counted for his Sunday best, but would, in other parts of the country, barely get him into the church stables: a dark blue suit only slightly worn at the knees, elbows, and seat, but an inch too short in the arms and an inch too long in the legs. The only thing keeping him from dragging the pants cuffs on the ground were his brown work boots which gave him just enough height to avoid fraying the legs. He wore a matching vest over a pale yellow shirt fastened at the neck with string tie.

"Oh, Caleb," the old man said with just a hint of disappointment in his voice, "I thought you were…" His voice trailed off a bit; then he blinked again and focused his attention more fully on his companion. "I thought you were someone else."

Caleb seemed to take this in stride. "Ardiss sent me out here to make sure you was ready."

Reverend Merle Tallison straightened himself, patted the scripture in his right pocket, then his prayer book in his left, and nodded.

"Yes, Caleb," he said, sounding more self-assured. "I believe we may begin now. Please have them bring the casket."

II.

"I know that my Redeemer liveth, and that He shall stand at the latter day upon the earth." As Rev. Tallison read from the prayer book, the pallbearers brought the casket to the gravesite. The congregation followed silently behind, Ardiss Drake limping at their head, his wife, and his chief deputy conspicuously absent, assisted to his place by his foster brother, Caleb.

"And though this body be destroyed, yet shall I see God." Rev. Tallison's voice caught a bit here, but no one seemed to notice. As they came to the gravesite, the congregation formed into rows three rows of six then spread out in a semicircle around the site, finding places in between the other graves and headstones.

"Whom I shall see for myself and mine eyes shall behold," he paused again here as if contemplating. The pall-bearers took this for a signal and began slowly to lower the casket into the grave.

"And not as a stranger." He finished weakly, but again, no one appeared to notice. Everyone seemed focused only on the casket as it sank into the ground. When this was done, Rev. Tallison turned to the congregation and smiled.

"The Lord be with you," he said.

"And with thy spirit," the congregation replied.

"Let us pray," Rev. Tallison waited until the shuffling sounds of heads bowing was receded before continuing:

"O God, whose beloved Son did take little children into his arms and bless them: Give us grace to entrust Garrett to thy never-failing care and love, and bring us all to thy heavenly kingdom; through thy Son Jesus Christ our Lord, who liveth and reigneth with thee and the Holy Spirit, one God, now and forever."

The congregation murmured their amens, and Rev. Tallison motioned for Ardiss and Caleb to step forward. He handed Ardiss the Bible from his right hand coat pocket, and the sheriff opened it to the Psalm he had marked.

"Psalm 109," Ardiss' voice had been soaked in whiskey and drug through gravel by a team of unbroken horses. "Hold not thy peace, O God of my praise; for the mouth of the wicked and the mouth of the deceitful are opened against me: they have spoken against me with a lying tongue. They compassed me about also with words of hatred; and fought against me without a cause. For my love, they are my adversaries. And they have rewarded me evil for good, and hatred for my love."

Rev. Tallison winced at the growing anger in Ardiss' voice. Yesterday, sitting opposite Ardiss in his office planning the service, he had argued against including this psalm, claiming that it was inappropriate for the occasion.

"Inappropriate?" Ardiss slammed his fist against his desk hard enough to splinter the wood. "You know what's inappropriate, Merle?"

When Merle didn't answer, Ardiss rose from his chair and leaned over the desk, casting a shadow over his rector and closest advisor. "It's inappropriate that that Irish bastard killed the boy in cold blood trying to leave town with my spic strumpet of a wife. It's inappropriate the boy's brother, who should by rights, now be my chief deputy, is off God-knows-where chasing the potato-eating son-of-a-bitch, when I need him here, now. It's inappropriate that that poor boy, thanks to his idol's lust and his brother's hot-headed insistence on vengeance, will have no family at his memorial. And it's God-damned inappropriate that the Indians have picked now, when my second deputy is off playing hide and go seek with my chief deputy, to start rumbling about ghost dances and war chants."

Ardiss' face had grown beet red, and spittle flew from the corners of his mouth. He began wheezing, grabbed at his groin, and sank, deflated, back into his chair.

"It's inappropriate," he declared quietly, having spent his energy in his brief explosion, "that I can no longer make water without weeping like a newborn wanting suck. No, Merle, we're using that Psalm."

"Then you will have to read it," Rev. Tallison said rising, "The Lord is mad enough at me as it is without adding poor taste to the mix."

"I would've insisted on it, Merle," Ardiss said quietly as the Rev. Tallison pulled his door closed and returned to his rectory.

And here we are, Rev. Tallison thought, subtly shaking his head. He appears to be carrying it off fairly well.

Indeed, Ardiss' voice seemed to grow stronger with each verse, but no less gravelly. "Set thou a wicked man over him: and let Satan stand at his right hand. When he shall be judged, let him be condemned: and let his prayer become sin. Let there be none to extend mercy unto him because he remembered not to show mercy, but persecuted the poor and needy man, that he might even slay the broken in heart."

Here, at a motion from Ardiss, Caleb, who had been steadfastly holding his brother's arm lest he lose his balance, released Ardiss and moved back a step, ready to step back should Ardiss' strength give out.

"But do thou for me, O GOD the Lord, for thy name's sake: because thy mercy is good, deliver thou me. For I am poor and needy, and my heart is wounded within me. My knees are weak through fasting, and my flesh faileth of fatness" Ardiss' voice cracked here, and his legs wavered ever so slightly. Caleb moved toward him, but Ardiss shook his head, and Caleb stepped back.

"Help me, O LORD my God," Here Ardiss looked to the heavens and screamed, resembling a shorter, stockier, and louder version of Rev. Tallison before the funeral. "Save me according to thy mercy. Let them curse: when they arise, let them be ashamed, but let thy servant rejoice!"

Ardiss slumped but did not stumble. Caleb stepped forward again, and this time, Ardiss allowed him to take him by the shoulders and lead him to his place in the congregation. As the two of them passed, Rev. Tallison could see tears making their way down the sheriff's face, but Ardiss' mouth was set and his jaw firm. "Irish fuckin' bastard," he mumbled as he handed the reverend back his bible and took his place.

III.

"Into thy hands, O merciful Savior, we commend thy servant Garrett," As he spoke, Rev Tallison slowly made the sign of the cross over the casket. "Acknowledge we humbly beseech thee, a sheep of thine own fold, a lamb of thine own flock. Receive him into the arms of thy mercy, into the blessed rest of everlasting peace, and into the glorious company of the saints in light."

"Amen," the congregation replied as one and slowly began to file past the grave, led by Ardiss and Caleb.

"In sure and certain hope of the eternal life," Rev. Tallison spoke as each member of the congregation dropped a handful of dirt on the casket, "we commend our brother Garrett, and we commit his body to the ground; earth to earth, ashes to ashes, dust to dust. The Lord bless him and keep him. The Lord lift up His countenance upon him and give him peace. Amen."

At this, the last of the congregation, Gilley the feeble-minded stable boy dressed in his best suit with his tie tied too long, dropped his dirt on the casket and stood smiling beatifically at the reverend. The rest of the congregation stood silently, waiting for Rev. Tallison's benediction before dispersing back to town and the rest of their day's responsibilities.

Rev. Tallison stared silently down at the dirt covered casket. Even with the whole town here, there was barely enough dirt to cover more than three quarters of the casket. He reached down for his own handful of dust. After he dropped his own dirt upon the casket, he turned his face to the congregation, smiled at Gilley, and raised his right hand to bless the crowd.

"Go in peace," he commanded, "to love and serve the Lord."

"Thanks be to God." With that, the congregation dispersed. Rev. Tallison watched as Caleb walked Ardiss back to the sheriff's residence, Ardiss clearly still cursing his best friend and his wife as Caleb nodded solemnly with each word and patted his brother's shoulder.

After everyone had left, Rev. Tallison, alone in the graveyard again, looked down once more on the casket.

Go in peace, boy, he thought reaching down another handful of dust. *When you arrive at the Gates, tell Him I'd listen if He'd speak again to me.* As he dropped his dirt upon the casket, a crow cawed in the distance three times then fell silent.

Gilley returned carrying a shovel. He had changed into a pair of denim pants and taken off his jacket. He still wore, however, his shirt and tie (though he had tucked the end of the tie into his pants. "You want I should finish burying Garrett now, Reverend?" he asked.

"Yes, Gilley," the reverend said looking towards the western edge of the graveyard where the crow had flown off earlier and in the direction of the recent call. "I think that would be best."

"Okey doke," the boy said and set to with the shovel.

Someone was stumbling into the graveyard: a boy not much younger than Garrett, towheaded and rail thin. He was leading a sway-backed mule that was almost as thin as Gilley's shovel. Rev. Tallison ran over to the boy, leaping over the grave markers as they got in his way, quite a feat for a man who'd not see seventy again, but he did it with the same energy he'd had as a lad of seven.

He managed to reach the boy as his mule fell over on its side, dragging the boy with it. Rev. Tallison caught him before he cracked his skull on one of the few stone markers in the grave, Luther Drake's.

"I've been looking all over for you, sir," the boy said, as he stared beyond Rev. Tallison's head. "My name's Percival Murratt, and I want you to make me a knight."

Afterword and Acknowledgements

This book has been almost twenty years in the making. In the mid 1990's, while researching for my Master's thesis in American literature, I came across an old college reader from 1968 titled *Heroes and Antiheroes: A Reader in Depth*. In it, editor Harold Lubin claimed that the cowboy was America's answer to England's knight in armor. He made a fairly convincing argument comparing, among other things, the so-called "code of the West" to the chivalric code of medieval times. The idea of how the Arthurian legends would have played out as a spaghetti Western immediately occurred to me and clanked around my head for several years until I finally put fingers to keyboard two years ago to hammer something out.

Oddly enough, I never cared for the Western as a genre until writing this book. Since beginning my research on it though, I have become a fan of *Little Big Man, True Grit, The Life and Times of Judge Roy Bean*, and the HBO series *Deadwood*.

However, I have been fascinated with Arthurian literature since almost as long as I've been reading. One of the first "big" books I ever read was a bowdlerized version of the King Arthur legends, Sidney Lanier's *The Boy's King Arthur*. My parents gave it to me because our family is descended from his in some way (I think his sister married into our family way back in the hereyonder, but I forget).

I later read Malory's *Le Morte d'Arthur* in middle school, but my love for all things Arthur really began in high school when I came across two books. In 10th grade, my first girlfriend, Laura Sears, lent me her copy of Marion Zimmer Bradley's *The Mists of Avalon* to read. This book did two things I had never seen before: it told the Arthur stories from the points of view of the women characters, and it made everyone, from Guinevere to Morgan le Fay sympathetic. I enjoyed the idea of telling the old tales from new perspectives, but I especially loved reading a story where there were no real bad guys, just misunderstood motives.

After that I read everything I could find about King Arthur, from Mary Stewart's *Merlin* series to T.H. White's *The Once and Future King*. I even found John Jake's attempt at a King Arhtur novel, *Excaliber!*, and read it, disappointed though I was that it wasn't the inspiration for John Boorman's film.

Then, as a senior in high school, I stumbled upon Richard Monaco's *Parsival* series, and it became my absolute favorite retelling of the grail legend. Monaco draws heavily from Eschenbachh's *Parzival*, but he adds a more realistic touch and modern sensibility to the characters, making his version seem oddly more mythic even as it works as a metaphor for modern man's struggle between materialism and spirituality, between obtaining power over the self or inflicting power over others.

When she lent me her copy of *The Mists of Avalon*, Laura told me she wanted me to dedicate my first fantasy novel to her. While this isn't a traditional fantasy, it is probably as close to a fantasy novel as anything I'll ever write. Sadly, however, Laura passed away a few years ago, and we had fallen out of touch long before that. I'm dedicating this first volume of a proposed quartet to her just in case somewhere on the shores of Avalon, where the time is always summer and the apples are all in bloom, she finds it.

I would also like to thank Richard Monaco, for his constantly nagging me to get on with the book. He once wrote a screenplay for a Western version of the Parsival story and saw it mangled beyond recognition by Hollywood, so I suspect he really wants to see someone who respects the source material do it without outside interference. Richard, I hope you like it at least a quarter of how much I like your *Parsival* books.

Finally, I want to thank my wife, Tina, for proofreading the manuscript, helping me design the cover, and listening patiently (or at least pretending to) while I ramble on at inopportune times about my book ideas. I'm afraid it's not over yet, darlin'. We got three more of these things to do.

ABOUT THE AUTHOR

Leverett Butts teaches composition and literature at the Gainesville campus of the University of North Georgia. His poetry and fiction have appeared in *Eclectic* and *The Georgia State University Review*. He is the recipient of several fiction prizes offered by the University of West Georgia and TAG Publishing. His first collection of short fiction, *Emily's Stitches: The Confessions of Thomas Calloway and Other Stories*, was nominated for the 2013 Georgia Author of the Year Award in Short Fiction. He lives in Temple, Georgia, with his wife, son, their Jack Russell terrier, and two cats (one is antisocial, but the other's just dead).